PREFACE

About a month after I moved into a rental property in Mountain House, California, a small community seventy miles from San Francisco, I dreamed a ghostlike figure of an Indian man with long black hair wearing fringed leather pants and no shirt running toward me down the hallway. He stopped short by the sliding glass door and said to me, "You can see me?"

I said "yes", and then he promptly turned to his right and disappeared through the sliding glass door. My dog growled and ran out of her dog door as if she was chasing something. This dream inspired me to begin researching the area I had just moved to.

looking up the history of Mountain House. The first line of the article read, "Native people have lived in this area for five thousand years." I started gathering all the information I could, doing extensive research on the subject of native people living in this area and about the Missions, even visiting Mission San Jose in Fremont, about twenty miles from my home. I came across a book that had newspaper articles on actual events that took place in the Central Valley of California, and one article contained an account of an event that took place in 1859. This is the story I weaved around that event.

CHEVEYO

The stillness of the morning was shattered by the squeals of laughing children. The women were at their morning tasks at campfires, preparing the morning meals. Cheveyo awakened, leaned up on one elbow, and poked his head out of a slit in the lodge. He filled his lungs with cool fresh air, squinting against the brightness of the sunlight stinging his eyes. The warm glow of slumber left him, and he was snapped awake when a panicking rabbit ran between the lodges, so close to him that he could reach out and touch it, followed by a deer with her doe.

"This is a good sign for the hunt today," Cheveyo said aloud as he slipped his moccasins onto his feet. Pushing the lodge cover aside, he jumped up and stepped out of the lodge.

He was about to run after the fleeing animals but was halted by Domona's soft voice. "Cheveyo, my love, you will have much time today to catch those. Right now you must eat so you have strength for the hunt."

Clutching her about the hips, he pulled her close to him, placing a kiss on her lips. He sat down near the fire and she handed

1

him his morning meal. He smiled up at her, taking note of her belly growing with their first child.

Suddenly the ground beneath him began to rumble. Standing up and dumping his meal to the ground, he looked at Domona.

Domona pointed to the west. "Look!" she cried.

He looked in the direction of her pointing. From the west, a cloud of brown haze filled the horizon, like the fog that rolls down the hillside on a damp morning. Within the dust cloud, rays of sunlight reflected off a thousand raised swords.

The thunderous sound approaching the village became louder until the marauding soldiers were upon them. With the force of a wave crashing on the shore, the horsemen reached the village. The conquering of the village was achieved swiftly. With raised swords slashing and horses stomping, the soldiers came, and the people scattered in all directions. Screaming natives ran for their lives to no avail. The soldiers were well versed in the job of capturing innocent people.

BRUNO

Bruno led his company of soldiers down the steep incline, with the targeted village in his sights. He sat tall in the saddle. He liked how his shoulder-length black hair blew in the wind as he rode. Though he was a young man, his leathery skin gave him an older appearance—the evidence of a hard life. His attention was focused on the job at hand—a very important one to the Crown and to God and his country. He raised his sword high and shouted the command to open flanks and spread out across the field. The army of soldiers led by Bruno headed full steam toward the village.

CHEVEYO

In the Council Lodge, Chief Enapy and five council members met. "Oh, Great Spirit, give strength to our warriors so that they may hunt well to fill our food stores for the winter that is coming."

Chief Enapy and the council members Liwanu, Tululi, Elsu, Wuyea, and Kono left the lodge and saw the people running and screaming. The chief looked at Kono with a puzzled look; he just shrugged his shoulders.

A young brave ran up to Chief Enapy and the council members standing at the council lodge. "Chief, come quickly!"

Chief Enapy, now seeing the attack on the village, shouted, "Take the women and children into hiding! Now!"

Cheveyo grabbed Domona's hand and started to run to the far side of the village. Before they could get even a few steps, a soldier on horseback abruptly cut off their path. Cheveyo nearly collided with the studded leather boot of a soldier. The soldier was Bruno.

Looking up at the soldier's weathered face, Cheveyo pulled Domona closer to his side. Without speaking a word, Bruno pointed to the center of the village, where the people were being forced to gather. Cheveyo, not wanting any harm to come to Domona and their unborn child, took her by the hand and led her toward the center of the village. Bruno, on horseback following the couple, watched the young pair. He observed the young couple and could see the love that the young Native woman had for her man.

Bruno, full of envy, had never felt that kind of love. He felt a yearning and a stirring in his loins for the young Native woman.

The village people were rounded up—all but the few who had refused or were not able to comply. Those had met with the cold steel of the soldier's blade.

Among those who met their demise was the oldest of the village, long revered as "the wise man." He lay bloodied on the ground. A baby, ripped from its mother's breast, had been tossed onto a rock, splitting its head open. An old woman had been mauled by the jaws of the vicious dogs that accompanied the soldiers. Another child had been tossed up into the air only to be impaled upon the steel blade of its holder. Among the dead was the old woman who was called "mother to the village."

Cheveyo stepped over the bloodied and brutalized bodies of the weak and defenseless people of his tribe—people he loved, his family. Domona walked, shrieking a death chant with tears running down her face, clutching Cheveyo's arm, and trying to avoid the pools of blood around all the dead bodies that littered the ground.

They reached the center of the village, where the people huddled in fear of these barbaric invaders who were destroying their homes and their lives.

Chief Enapy and the five council members stepped forward. "I am chief of these people. I demand to know why you have come here to harm us. We are a peaceful people. We have done you no harm. Leave us now before more blood is spilled."

Bruno rode up and slithered off of his horse. He stood facing the Chief, his cold, beady eyes staring into the pain-filled eyes of Chief Enapy.

Without looking away, he shouted an order. "Jose!" Bruno waved his hand and a native appeared. He wore pantaloons with silver studs along the pant, a vest of silver meshing, a silver helmet upon his head, and a sword holder about his hip. This was the same manner of dress of all the soldiers present. Jose stepped forward and began translating every word Bruno said.

"I am Captain Bruno Diaz. m a representative of the land of Spain. I have been sent here to claim this land in the name of Her Royal Highness and God. I offer you a chance at a new life—an easier way of life. Where food is plenty and you won't have to hunt. No more starving in the cold winter months, no more failure to find the sustenance that you need to feed your people. Come with me to a place that is paradise. You will be taught how to grow your own food, and we will give you shelter. You will be taught the way of our God. Come with me peacefully now. No further harm will come to you and your people."

Chief Enapy took a step forward, facing the translator and speaking to Bruno. "I am Enapy. I am chief to these people. Our fathers have lived on these lands for thousands of years. My people have lived this way of life that has kept us alive and happy. A way that follows a peaceful path. One that we do not want to and will not give up."

Bruno, with lines of fatigue appearing on his weathered face, gritted his yellow teeth. He took in a deep breath, his impatience visible as he barked out a command to the interpreter. "Take them!"

The soldiers surrounding the people jumped at Bruno's order. They grabbed and bound the hands of the chief and five council members with leather straps.

Soldiers began to disassemble lodges, leaving only the center poles, strong and true, sticking up out of the ground. The council members were tied two to a pole, and Chief Enapy was tied to another.

Bruno approached the chief with his interpreter and asked him once again, this time in a more pleading way, "Will you lead your people to come with us to a better way of life that we are offering you? Or will you stay here and pay the consequences?"

Chief Enapy stood his ground and, with his head held high, spoke to his people. "I, Chief Enapy, love all of you like my children. If I must die to keep you from this new way, than it shall be done. Know that I will be with you in spirit." He turned to Bruno and said, "No, we will not go with you. Now leave us!"

Bruno, now red-faced, angrily bellowed a command to his soldier. Two soldiers ran off and quickly came back in seconds with the tall tule that had been the roofs of the lodges in their arms. The tule were cut into kindling swiftly and placed waist-high around the council members, Tukuli, Liwanu, Wuyea, Elsu, and Kono.

The people stood by silently, watching, frozen in fear. Bruno, standing next to Chief Enapy, raised his sword high above his head, and with a stroke of his arm the blade came down with a whooshing sound. Chief Enapy's face winced in silent pain. A red streak appeared from his throat to his groin. For a brief moment, Chief Enapy looked down at his body and then back up. There were gasps and screams from the people as they witnessed Chief Enapy's torso split open; his blood and intestines spilled out onto the ground at his feet. Chief Enapy's face turned an ashen white, and he slumped forward against the leather straps that held him to the pole.

Bruno barked another order, and a soldier jumped to the command. He picked up the end piece of the Chief's entrails that lay in the bloodied dirt at his feet. The soldier circled the Chief several times, making a mock rope of the entrails. Soldiers came forward with more tule branches and laid them at Chief's Enapy's feet. Bruno called out another order, and still more cut tules were placed at the feet of Chief Enapy, making it waist high. One more soldier came forward with a fiery torch. The tule were set afire at the feet of Chief Enapy. Next, the kindling at the feet of the council members was set aflame. Smoke filled the air, stinging the eyes of the disbelieving captives.

The fire rose up the kindling surrounding the tied up council members. Tukuli and Elsu began writhing backward against the poles in an attempt to get away from the advancing flames. Kono and Wuyea were wailing and chanting a prayer to the

Great Spirit, while Liwanu stood bravely with his eyes looking up to the sky.

More tules were piled onto the fires, and the heat made Bruno step back. The flames were white hot now, and the hair was burned off the heads of the council members. Their cries of agony filled the air.

Soon, all were coughing and gasping for the breath that would sustain them only to sputter and wheeze. Huge blisters formed on the skin of the captives, and as the fire rose the blisters popped, and the fluid sizzled as the skin around it charred.

More tules were piled on. The flames were too high now to see the writhing men. The village people began to chant and wail and cry in an agony of their own. Some of the women grabbed handfuls of hair and pulled it out in large chunks.

As the charred remains of the chief and council members smoldered, the people were gathered into two groups. The women were separated from the men.

All were surrounded by soldiers. Iron chains were applied to the necks of the native men.

Bruno mounted his horse to observe. Up on that horse, above all the people scurrying about, he felt powerful. He could also watch the lovely native woman who had caught his eye. He noticed that she stood tall and slender, a head taller than the rest. She had long, black silken hair and a face of beautiful innocence. She noticed him staring at her and quickly looked away.

A cold iron brace was applied to Cheveyo's neck. It was pulled taut and dug into his neck. Chains connected the braces on the men from neck to neck. There was long line of chains that bound him to his brothers. The men were ordered to start walking. The chains were restrictive; Cheveyo had to adjust his pace to a rhythm that he maintained so as not to be pulled down to the ground.

Soldiers on horseback surrounded the lines of captives. The native women walked in front. There was no hope of escape.

As they walked through the field toward the west, Cheveyo looked back at his village. The lodges were ablaze, and he could see bodies of his people on the bloodied ground. The food stores were pillaged, and empty baskets that had contained food were strewn about.

Seething anger replaced the sorrow he had felt in his heart. With each step he took away from his home, that anger grew stronger and stronger. He made a vow to himself that someday he would escape and have vengeance on these invaders.

They walked all day in the heat. Cheveyo's lips became dry, and his throat was parched. He needed water; still they walked. He worried about how Domona was doing. He could see her ahead with the other women of his village. He wasn't the only one watching the lovely Domona. Bruno kept her in his sights as well.

They reached the canyon of the Altamont Pass, a foothill of the taller Mount Diablo in the distance. Alongside the path was a stream of gently rolling water in a creek bed carved out from years of raging floods. The water looked so inviting. Cheveyo looked up at the rounded walls of the canyon surrounding him. The golden grass swayed in the breeze, and the bales of tumbleweeds rolled by. He had been this way once before, in his youth, when he went with a hunting party to the edge of the earth where the great water was.

Kosumi, who was bound in front of Cheveyo, was growing weary. He was not a strong man; they were brothers in spirit only. Both had grown up without a father. Cheveyo's father had been killed by a rampaging bear on a hunt. Kosumi's father had died in a stampede of horses. He and Kosumi had both been raised by Chief Enapy. Cheveyo had always looked out for

Kosumi because Kosumi was the weaker of the two. Cheveyo loved him and would do anything for him. At last, the men were finally allowed to stop and drink from the stream that ran along the path they were walking.

The heat of the day increased, and the walking became more difficult. As they trekked through the valley on the other side of the Altamont Pass, Kosumi stumbled and fell to the ground. Cheveyo quickly grabbed him by the arms and pulled him up. But Cheveyo's efforts were useless. By the time they got through the passage, Kosumi was dragging his feet, and sweat was pouring from his body.

A short time later, Kosumi fell to his knees. Cheveyo grabbed at his body to pull him up again. The soldier who guarded the flanks charged up to Kosumi, who was sitting on his haunches in the golden grass.

The soldier jumped off of his horse and stood over the whimpering Kosumi. "Get up!" he ordered.

Kosumi just sat on the ground and sobbed. "I can't go any longer! I'm tired and thirsty!"

The angered soldier looked down at Kosumi. "You're pathetic!" He took his knife from its sheath, the sun reflecting off of the blade blinding Cheveyo momentarily. The soldier snatched a handful of Kosumi's hair. With a stroke of his knife, he lowered the blade and ran it across the neck of Kosumi. His throat was cut from ear to ear. A gush of blood washed down the front of his body. Cheveyo tried to scream to stop this madness, but he was pushed to the ground, and with the chain about his neck, he was stuck with the others who were tethered to him. Kosumi's lifeless body slumped to the earth, causing a puff of dust to drift up into the air.

Other soldiers, seeing the commotion, came running with their weapons waving and shouting commands to the captives to start walking. Cheveyo started walking, staring at the empty bloodied neck iron swinging in the air and providing a constant reminder of his loss with each step.

As the sun sank lower into the western sky, the group stopped at the river's edge. They were allowed to drink and would rest here for the night. Cheveyo drank the cool water with his cupped hands.

He settled himself onto the dead grass. He stared coldly at Bruno and made a note of everything around him so that no matter how far the conquistadors took them, he would find his way back.

The sun greeted Cheveyo the next morning as it rose over the distant hills. The neck iron was cold against his neck. Cheveyo sat up, the jingling chain and the empty neck iron attached to it reminding him of the loss of his brother. He looked around for Domona. Seeing her and the other women at the bank of the creek, he felt a little at ease; she was as safe as could be under the circumstances.

The command was given and all got to their feet and began walking. The direction they were being led was unfamiliar to Cheveyo. The farthest he had traveled was going to the edge of the world to the big water, where they had caught much fish. It was there that he had found the most beautiful seashell. He'd brought it home to Domona and made a necklace from it. That necklace was her most treasured item, now gone…everything was gone. He told himself that that he must now pay close attention to the present in order to see where they would end up and to the future to find a way home.

At noon, when the sun was directly overhead, he looked toward the mountain called Diablo. He made a mental note that it would be to his back on the day he would escape his captors. The brush grew taller, and some trees dotted the landscape. He wished he could sit under one of those trees to rest in the shade. They were traveling toward some high hills, and he wondered if they would go up those hills or look for a pass between them.

The warm afternoon sun beat down with just a few wispy clouds in the sky. A gentle breeze carried a strange and unpleasant smell that was unfamiliar to Cheveyo…the smell of cattle. In the distance, he could see some cows grazing. At first, a few dotted the horizon, and then they became more numerous as they walked.

They came to the edge of a vast field of corn. The stalks of corn were as tall as a man as they gently waved in the wind. In between the stalks were native men and women with tools tending the ground around the base of the corn.

As he passed by the cornfield, he looked at the workers. He was amazed at the condition they were in. The clothes they were wearing were dirty and torn. Their faces were ghostlike and lifeless. It was as if they were under a spell. One of the workers, a native man bending over with a tool in hand, looked up at Cheveyo as he walked by. Cheveyo was haunted by the emptiness within the eyes of the worker. The soldiers were all around the workers in the field—guarding them and pushing them to work harder. The cracking of the whip and a shouting of the guard to keep working was heard.

There was more walking until finally they came to rest at a long lodge made of the thickest of tule stalks with thinner tules used for roofing. Passing these lodges, Cheveyo noticed some women and children busy with various tasks. They continued walking until they passed a tall building made of brick that was painted bright white. The brightness of the white building was such that he had to squint his eyes to avoid blindness. There was a bell and a cross made of wood at the top of this building. Passing this building, Cheveyo noticed many native men busy at work making the clay mud bricks that these outer buildings consisted of. The workers looked up at his group and then at the soldiers guarding them and back to work they went. They too were gaunt and had that haunted, lifeless look in their eyes.

Some of the native men were bringing straw to the brick makers. Then the bricks were carried to a different area where another building was being built. The workers struggled to keep up the frenzied pace set by the soldiers guarding them. The brick building was the largest one yet. Much larger than the council chambers of Cheveyo's village.

They stopped at the center of the compound. Here there were many soldiers engaged in various acts of battle training. They were led to stand in front of a wooden door of a smaller white brick building.

The captives were lined up in front of this building in rows of ten. Thirty new captives in all. The neck irons were removed one by one. The sound of the chains as they hit the ground was a sound that sent chills down Cheveyo's spine—the sound of the end of freedom as he had known it.

Cheveyo was relieved to have the weight removed from his body. The iron had scraped at his neck, causing the skin to rub raw and blister. The chains were collected by a native who was dressed in the same manner as those in the fields—white pantaloons and white shirts tied with a colorful sash about the waist with leather sandals on their feet and a hat made of straw.

The women were taken to a lodge at the end of the compound. Cheveyo observed that it was heavily guarded and locked up tight. He could hear some soldiers barking orders in a language that was foreign to him.

Bruno rode up on his horse, dismounted, and went inside the smaller brick building. He stomped the dust off of his boots as he stepped on the wooden planks leading to the doorway, went inside, and turned to the right. There he found a large table with fruit and a pitcher of water. He helped himself to the water and a handful of grapes. Turning to the left, he saw Father Anthony, dressed in a long black hooded robe with a hemp sash around his waist. The padre sat at a table that he used as a desk, writing in a journal. He continued to write in his journal for a few minutes as Bruno stood in front of his desk, patiently waiting to be addressed. Setting down his writing implement, the padre looked up at Bruno.

"That was a relatively fast trip; I hope it went well," Father Anthony said to Bruno.

Bruno shifted his weight from foot to foot. "Your Grace, we have brought back thirty able-bodied men and twenty-five women and children. We had to take the village by force, killing the chief, and I regret that many were slaughtered."

The padre looked up at Bruno. His face reddened as he spoke. "If you can't control your men, I will get someone who will!" the padre said as he stood.

Fidgeting with the helmet he held with both hands, he waited for his opportunity to speak. A bead of sweat broke out on Bruno's forehead, and he looked down at the floor. "Your Grace, it has been very difficult keeping these men in line. The caliber of the men we recruit now is just not what it was when I began this job years ago. The men now are coming from the South, no longer from the Homeland. They are ill-mannered and not much more civilized than the savages we capture, but I need men, and this is all I can get."

The padre walked across the room to peer out the window. He observed the new captives silently for a moment and then with a calmer voice explained, "I have a mission here, and that is to take these wild pagan animals and transform them into good, righteous Christians. It makes my job all the more difficult if they enter this Holy place angry. They fight it all the more." The padre went back to his desk and sat down with a sigh. "Well, anyway, it is done. Now send San Juan to me, I need him to translate." The padre waved Bruno off.

The black-robed padre arose and walked outside of the adobe building into the warmth of the afternoon sun. Bruno trailed behind him. San Juan, the native interpreter, ran up alongside the padre. The padre, Bruno, and San Juan faced the group of new captives.

"Hello, my children, I am Father Anthony. I will be your teacher and guide." San Juan the interpreter repeated word for word for the padre. "You are here today for a purpose: to be transformed into a child of God. To live a life that he has for all his people. A civilized way of life. You will learn to grow food and know God's word and how to be good citizens. I will teach you to live on the righteous path that God has laid out for all of his children. You will now be referred to as neophytes, because you are like newly born from this day forward." After his speech, the padre turned and went back into his adobe office.

Bruno turned to the captives. He ordered San Juan to translate for him. "You are here now. Do not attempt to escape. Do not make a fool of me by trying. Should you decide to try an escape, I will hunt you down, and I will not stop until you are recaptured. Let me show you what I do to those who escape when I catch them. Here is what you will face upon recapture. Here is what will become of you."

Bruno yelled a command toward a barn area that faced the center of the compound, and a group of neophytes came out, surrounded by soldiers. Two of the native men were bound by leather straps around their hands. One of the escapees was dragged over to a stump of a tree. His bindings were untied, and he was pushed to the ground in a kneeling position in front of the stump. A soldier grabbed the escapee's arm. Two other soldiers held the escapee in place as his arm was made to rest on the stump. A soldier standing over the kneeling escapee looked over at Bruno, who gave a nod of his head. The solder raised a tool used for cutting corn stalks and brought it down onto the wrist of the kneeling escapee. The escapee gave a cry like a wounded animal in the wild, holding up his arm in shock as blood spurted out of the severed limb and his severed hand lay twitching in the dirt. The neophyte went limp and was dragged back to the barn.

"This is the punishment of an escapee. If you escape once, you get the whip. Twice and you will lose a limb." Bruno said with a cynical tone.

Two soldiers were escorting another neophyte by the arms. They dragged him to where the group was standing. His hands were bound in front of him. One of the solders raised the neophyte's bound hands up to a hook on a pole in the ground in the center of the compound. The neophyte's shirt had been removed. A soldier handed a whip to Bruno, who swung it high into the air. The whip came down with a whistling sound and a crack that was equal to thunder. A deafening cry of pain came from the escapee. Several more times, the whistling, cracking, screaming sound rang out until the man tied to the pole fell unconscious. Two solders grabbed the beaten neophyte, and another untied his hands and dragged him away, blood dripping down his shredded back.

Bruno barked another order and several soldiers came running, surrounding the group of neophytes. They were led to a large tulle building, and each was given a blanket. Cheveyo shuffled into the lodge and found an empty spot at the end of the lodge. He placed his blanket down on the ground and lay his head down, throwing his arm over his eyes. His body felt so heavy with the fatigue that overcame him that he fell fast asleep.

THE MISSION

The clanging of a bell woke Cheveyo out of a sound sleep. He did not know how he could sleep at all with the happenings of the day before. A flurry of soldiers raced into the lodge, and orders were given for everyone to get up and get to the chapel. Like sheep, they were herded to the tall white building and instructed by an interpreter to sit on wooden benches that were in rows. They received their first lesson. Cheveyo looked down at the leather-bound book that was placed in his hand. He opened it and flipped through page after page of words—words that were foreign to him but ones that he would later learn. He listened to the padre's speech. He vowed to himself to comply and not stand out so that when the time came for escape he would notice.

When the lesson was completed, the group was led past the center of the compound to the dining building and given a bowl of food and a piece of bread. It was something that Cheveyo had never experienced before. It was a mush made of corn and beans. It had a different smell...not bad, but different. Hunger took over at this point, and he quickly ate the gruel and bread that was given to him. The order was given and he was led outside. Once outside, he was directed into a group for his daily task. He looked around and saw a group of native women from his village. He needed to see Domona.

He looked around for her. Then he saw her from across the compound, looking so beautiful, taller than the other women. He smiled at her. Her protruding belly was a reminder of the life they had created. She smiled back at him.

Just then he felt a hand on his back, shoving him forward and making him lose his balance. Stumbling to the ground, he rolled over to look into the face of Bruno. Bruno pointed to a soldier and with a loud voice shouted for Cheveyo to go to the group that was being taken to the field. He would be tending the cornfields, just like the workers he had seen when he'd first arrived. He was given a hoe and marched out to the field.

Bruno caught a glimpse of Domona across the compound too. The sight of her made his heart flutter. He smiled at her. She quickly looked away.

Cheveyo was a fast learner. He began picking up some words that were spoken by the soldiers. He was a good student too and learned his daily lessons, unlike some of the unlucky ones who could not grasp the words or the lessons being taught; they were whipped daily. With the padre's teachings and the soldier's harsh treatment, he quickly learned that the best way to gain favors was to do what they wanted and do it well.

One evening after the evening meal, Cheveyo and other neophytes were in their lodge. The doors burst open and soldiers came rushing in. Bruno, standing at the entrance with a smirk on his face, pointed to a man lying on his mat next to Cheveyo. The soldiers yanked the man by the arms and dragged him out the door. Out into the dark of night, Cheveyo and several others crept to the door and watched as the neophyte was dragged out and tied to a post, screaming in pain at the lashings that he was receiving.

Scurrying back to their sleeping mats, the group of watchers fell and lay still. They didn't even want to breathe for fear that the now almost nightly beatings that were occurring would happen to them. The soldiers dragged the beaten man into the lodge and dumped him onto his mat. There he lay still.

The morning light shone into the building through the tule roof, waking Cheveyo. He lay on his side, facing the man who had been beaten the night before. "Hey, how are you faring?" Cheveyo whispered to him.

The man did not respond.

"Hey, Amigo!" Cheveyo said, louder this time. Sitting up he reached his hand to shake the man lying on his stomach. He could see the shredded skin and much blood loss. The man did not move. Cheveyo shook the man again and still no movement. He put his hand on the man's ice cold face, sending a chill down his spine.

The bell began to toll, and everyone in the lodge obediently stood and fell in line to go to the morning lesson.

After the long day in the field, with an aching back and blistered hands, Cheveyo hurried to the hall where supper was being served. He had to see Domona. He longed to hold her in his arms and looked forward to meeting his child.

Cheveyo was not the only one who desired to see Domona. Bruno lurked in the shadows to catch a glimpse of the raven-haired beauty. His loins stirred at the sight of her. Then, seeing her smile at Cheveyo, he was full of rage.

"I want her to notice *me*," Bruno said to himself.

The long days passed. Cheveyo worked hard and studied at the padre's lessons. Then one day, Domona was not at supper. Worry overcame him. He risked a lashing for sneaking to the heavily guarded women's dorm and shouting up to a window inquiring about his wife. Had anyone seen her? Worry kept him awake all that night.

The next day at breakfast, Cheveyo was happily surprised to see Domona. She had a little bundle in her arms. Cheveyo put risk aside and walked over to his wife and new baby girl. He gently took the baby girl from his wife and gazed down at her beauty. Cradling her in his arms and then holding her up high above his head to the Great Spirit, he gave thanks for a healthy baby and safe delivery. Then he said aloud, "We will call her Luna—she has the beauty of the moon and the power that comes from it."

Bruno, seeing this, charged over to Cheveyo. Holding his whip up in the air, he bellowed, "Get back to your place, neophyte!"

Cheveyo gently kissed his baby on the forehead and gave her back to Domona. Returning to his place among the other neophytes, he felt the sting of the whip as it ripped at his back. He was so full of joy at the birth of his daughter that a few lashes from the whip were worth it. He was now a father.

Cheveyo took to the field right away. He raked through the weeds, tilled the soil, and tended to the growing of the corn and beans until his hands were blistered and torn. His back aching, he never stopped doing the best job he could. Even with his studies, he picked up on the language of the soldiers, mostly so he could hear and understand what they spoke of.

After each day of back-breaking work, he would hurry to supper to catch a glimpse of Domona—just to see her beautiful smile. He noticed Bruno was always there watching her too.

Cheveyo noticed some couples living together in small apartments that were simple huts made of tulle branches just behind the main compound. He asked others working alongside him in the field how he could get an apartment like that and be reunited with his wife and child. He learned that to get one, a couple had to be married in a ceremony in the church.

Cheveyo wanted this more than anything for now, to be with his family. He did not like that they were separated. It was forbidden to even speak to his wife, so just looking at her smile was all that he had.

The women's dormitory was a tall white building with very thick walls where they were locked up every night. The windows had iron bars, and the building was surrounded on all sides by a thick grove of cactus that stood as high as the wall itself. It was heavily guarded by solders day and night, so it was impossible to speak to Domona.

After the evening meal one day, the neophytes were called to gather in the center of the compound. There in the center was Awok, a brother from Cheveyo's village he had known since childhood. Awok, now known as Don Jose, his new baptized name, was tied to the whipping post and was to be punished for escaping. The sound of the lash snapping as it ripped the flesh off of Don Jose's back made Cheveyo cringe. He could not watch as his brother was being punished. He could not take hearing the painful screams that reminded him of the anger that lay dormant within him as he turned and fled to his lodge.

The days wore on. Cheveyo moved on to other daily tasks. There was no task he could not do and do well. He went from the field to the tannery, where he took hides that had been soaked in a salt solution and left to dry and scraped off the hair with a knife. This made the leather smooth and free of marks. He had this task for a while.

He would see Domona walking with Luna to her position in the weaving area at the evening supper. He longed to have a ceremony and be married in the church, but this was difficult, for the padre was frequently absent, since his duties took him to other nearby Missions. There were many Missions that dotted Alta California.

In the meantime, he watched as his beautiful little girl, Luna, toddled around behind Domona as she walked from her work area to the women's dormitory. Every day, he needed to see her.

BRUNO

Bruno rode sleepily atop his horse. He had set out early in the morning on a trip to capture runaways. Some of these were repeat offenders. They would pay severely this time, Bruno thought. He was growing weary of these trips.

He was also growing weary of the soldiers he commanded. The quality of the men used to be so good. Now, however, they were shiftless, lazy, and untrustworthy. He dreamed of the day when he could hang up his uniform and settle in a nice ranchero with that little native woman, Domona. He dreamed of a having home with Domona as he rode. A stirring in his loins drew his attention back to the moment, and looking around, he hoped nobody he was traveling with had noticed. Feeling uneasy, he adjusted his pantaloons.

The searing sun beating down on him made him surly. The sweat pouring off of his forehead stung his eyes as his horse lumbered along the dry sagebrush that dotted the plain.

Suddenly, up ahead, Bruno could see a faint movement. His eyes focused on the horizon, and sure enough, the runaways were walking through the plain.

A grin broke out on his face as he kicked the sides of his horse and pushed the horse to a full gallop. With him and a few of his soldiers at his side, they picked up speed and in a short time were upon the runaways.

The runaways, four in all, turned to see Bruno and company coming at them at full speed and began to scatter and run.

Bruno went after one, pulling a rope off of his saddle. He was proficient at lassoing cattle. He had learned it from the caballeros who worked the livestock at the Mission and he was quiet proud of himself. Taking the rope and spinning it around above his head, he tossed it, missing its mark. Stopping his horse and gathering up his rope, he made a second attempt at the running escapee.

The rope fell around the escapee, and Bruno yanked up hard on the rope, securing it tightly around the neophyte and knocking him to the ground. Bruno jumped off his horse and tied the neophyte's hands with a leather strip.

"You can't run from me. I will always find you and return you!"

Bruno got back up on his horse, holding the rope still wrapped around the escapee. The other escapees joined the one held by Bruno.

Bruno tied the end of the rope to his saddle, and they began the ride back to the Mission. Bruno's horse trotted along at just the right speed so that the escapee had to almost run to keep from tripping and being dragged.

When they got back to the Mission, Bruno corralled the escapees in the center of the compound. Their hands were shackled to posts and soldiers held the head of the first neophyte.

Bruno approached him, pulling his knife out of its sheath with a snarling expression, and said, "So you keep running away, but each time I will find you and bring you back, and each time your punishment will worsen. With that, he took his knife, held it to the escapee's nose, and sliced it off at the tip. The blood dripped down into the man's mouth and chin as he screamed in agony. Bruno tossed the runaway's nose tip to the dirt and stepped on it, smashing it into the ground.

The next escapee stood defiant. "You can do whatever to my body, but you cannot harm my soul!"

Bruno shrugged his shoulders, put the knife to his nose, and cut off the tip. The next escapee in line was shaking. "Please, I have not done this before, do not punish me so severely."

Bruno looked at the whimpering escapee, He put his knife up to the forehead of this escapee and carved a cross.

"Well, make this your last time," Bruno said as he wiped the blood on the escapee's pant leg, turned, and walked away.

CHEVEYO

Cheveyo become very proficient at the language that the padre and, more importantly, the soldiers spoke. This gave him an advantage above others. Soon he was able to go with the teams of workers to the neighboring Missions to trade hides for sugar and salt. The day-long trips broke the monotony.

At night, after the retiring bell when all were tucked away in their beds and the final check by the soldiers was done, Cheveyo and some other neophytes would sneak out to the fields to build a shrine and worship the Great Spirit, which they had grown up believing in. They knew full well that if they were caught it would mean getting a lashing.

These meetings helped with the rampant depression that plagued the neophytes. Cheveyo watched helplessly as the people he knew from his village, withered away with poor diet, hard work, and harsh living conditions, perish and die, only to be replaced by new captives.

Bruno and his solders went on regular raids, returning with natives from all over the territory. Suicide was becoming more common among the neophytes.

Cheveyo would seek out the returning captives, the escapees, to gather information about their escape—such as what route they took and how they were found. He discovered that it was easy to escape but avoiding being recaptured was the hard part.

Escaping was heavy on his mind now, but he could not leave Domona and Luna. They were always either locked up in the women's dormitory or under the watchful eyes of the soldiers.

Luna had reached the age that she was with other children her age for a short time each day. He would see her going to her lessons. His little girl was growing up without him. This made him sad.

Cheveyo gained the trust of the caballeros. His task was to tend to the soldiers' horses. He especially liked this job. This also included taking care of the mules that drove the padre's cart. Cheveyo saw the padre often now as he got the cart ready that would take the padre to the other Missions. He thought perhaps this would give him an opportunity to speak to the padre about getting an apartment with Domona.

Happiness overtook him as he walked back to the men's lodge. Cheveyo had not felt this optimistic in a long time. Not since he was living free at his village...which was now just a distant memory.

He entered the lodge to see a group of his native brothers huddled in a circle around a native he had not seen before. The native stood up. His short stature was compensated by his confident manner. He looked like a leader. He motioned for Cheveyo to come join the group.

"Come sit with us. I am Jose Manuel, the new alcalde. I will represent you to the soldiers and the padre," the man said to Cheveyo. The alcalde was responsible for overseeing the neophytes.

Cheveyo pondered for just a moment. "Yes, I will join you." He sat with the group until it was time to go to the evening meal.

Later that night, Cheveyo was awakened by a whisper in his ear. It was Odakota. "Hey, we are going to the field—are you coming with us tonight?" Cheveyo shook the sleep from his head, got up, and followed the group out the door. They crept along the walls until they were well clear of the compound out past the fields to a clearing that they used for their worship. His eyes focused enough in the dark that he could see the makeshift shrine consisting of a pile of rocks, feathers, beads, shells, and silken sashes. The neophytes gathered around this to worship the Great Spirit. Jose Manuel started to chant. The others joined in until there was a harmony of chanting by the group, all in worship to the Great Spirit. Cheveyo could feel the warmth grow inside, and he stood up and, in full celebration, chanted and sang the song of their ancestors and danced around the pile of stones, shells, beads, and feathers. They did this until signs of early light began to peek over the horizon.

Cheveyo felt full of the light of the Great Spirit. He quietly snuck back into his lodge and, exhilarated, lay his head down to rest until the morning service of the lessons.

The following evening, Jose Manuel approached Cheveyo. "We are going to escape from this place. Come with us. If we all leave at once, they cannot stop us. So come join us. Tomorrow, just after morning meal, we will rise up and just walk out. You can be part of this too. They can't come after all of us."

Cheveyo pondered this. "I will let you know." In his heart he knew he could not leave without his wife and daughter.

Cheveyo's other job was the making of the tallow. He was proficient in this as he took the fat from the slaughtered cattle and churned it into soap that was sold to the soldiers' wives. The tallow had many other uses and was also shuttled to the other Missions. It was even transported to the port, where it was put on large ships and sent to far off lands.

Cheveyo was quickly assigned to drive the cart piled high with tanned hides and containers of supplies to the harbor, where it was loaded into cargo ships. This was a good assignment for Cheveyo until the rainy season. The mud was too thick on the trail for the carts to use, so piles of hides had to be carried atop one's head and walked the five long miles to the harbor. The job was not a favorite of his.

Close to the tannery were the pastures and pens where the cows were kept. Cheveyo soon got a position cleaning out the pens. Then he graduated to the horse stables. The horses were abundant in number, so much so that horses were slaughtered regularly to keep control of the herd. Horse meat was then sold to the soldiers' wives.

BRUNO

Bruno was out on the road again. This time he had headed south to a Mission that ran along the coast of California with a stop in Monterey, the Mission's headquarters. There he stayed at the rancheria that housed the soldiers and their families. The wife of one of the soldiers there was quiet and accommodating while her husband was on duty. Bruno could still smell the scent of her. As he rode his horse back to his Mission, his thoughts were of their night of passion.

As he approached his home Mission, he could not believe his eyes. There, streaming out of the entrance toward the hills, were hundreds of neophytes—men, women, and children—running from the Mission. Pushing and shoving in a large bunch, they made their way out into the open and then fanned out and scurried in all directions.

Bruno stopped and just stared at the scene that was unfolding before him. There was no way he could stop the flow, let alone capture all these runaways.

Kicking the sides of his horse, he went into a full gallop. Stopping his horse at the church, he slid off his horse and ran into the office. "Your Grace, what has happened here today?"

The padre was standing by the window with his hands clasped behind his back. "Come in, Bruno," he said with a heavy sound to his voice. "I do not understand why they run from this place, from me! I give them food, I give them shelter, I have taught them to be civilized human beings! Why do they betray me?"

Bruno stood fumbling with his vest buttons. "I cannot explain it, your Grace." He hoped the padre would not turn around.

Turning around, the padre looked dejected. With a sigh he said, "It seems that I have failed what I have set out to do. My children have abandoned me, and my soldiers leave here as soon as they serve their commitment. What am I to do, Bruno?"

"Should I go after them, Your Grace?" Bruno sheepishly asked.

"No" said the padre, "it would be useless to do so. We will double up the workload of the ones who are left here. Also, some of the lower ranking officers will have to do work details. We must keep this Mission functioning."

"But Your Grace," Bruno stammered, "who will keep the remaining neophytes in line if the soldiers are busy working?"

The padre turned to look out the window again. With his back to Bruno, he said, "It must be done or our whole purpose here will have been for naught."

"Yes, Your Grace." He turned and walked out the door. "This will put me in bad favor with my men," Bruno mumbled to himself.

One day when Cheveyo was in the stable washing down a horse, he was approached by Bruno. "You." Bruno pointed to him. "I have heard that you have learned my language and can speak it quite well; is this true?"

Cheveyo, who always stayed clear of Bruno, was taken aback by the direct approach from him. Gaining his composure, he spoke back to Bruno in a fluent smooth response as if he had spoken it all his life. "Yes, sir, I can."

Bruno and Cheveyo stood face to face. Bruno studied Cheveyo's face and noticed for the first time what a handsome man he was. He was as tall as himself, with a strong build and chiseled facial features. His eyes were light. He could see what Domona saw in him. No wonder that little beauty was devoted to him.

Bruno spoke up. "I need someone who can speak dual languages to help the doctor that comes once a month. He has requested an interpreter, and you will do. Come with me."

Bruno led Cheveyo to the building next to the chapel, to a room that had a cot in the middle of it and a man in a white coat who had his back to them.

"Is that you, Bruno?" the doctor asked as he turned around.

Dr. Ned Brown was a short man with gray thinning hair and spectacles resting on his nose. He was a kind man and cared about his patients. He saw anyone who was in need of care. The soldiers were the first to be seen and then any neophytes who ventured forth. The neophytes were reluctant to seek the white man's healer, preferring the magical powers of their own Shaman, whom they secretly went to in the dark of night.

At first, Cheveyo cleaned the room that was used as a makeshift clinic. He cleaned the doctor's instruments and threw out the bloodied bandages. He was very helpful to Dr. Brown as an interpreter. He learned a lot working with the doctor. One of the biggest complaints from the soldiers who came to see the doctor was sores on their genitals. Cheveyo listened as one particular soldier came to the clinic with sores on his genitals and blister-like rash on his torso.

Dr. Brown took one look at him and sighed. "You have an advanced case of the syphilis," he said.

The soldier looked up at Dr. Brown with a worried look on his face asked, "Will I die from this, Doc?"

Dr. Brown took out a brown bottle from his bag that sat on the table next to him. "You have the syphilis. It is caused by having intercourse with a dirty woman. You will not die from it, but there is no cure. I can only give you something to take the discomfort away. Furthermore, don't have any relations while you have any visible sign of these sores. If you do and it results in a pregnancy, the child would possibly be born blind. I have seen this with my own eyes. A baby born with white eyes. Blind as a bat. Here, take this and drink it twice a day until it is gone." The doctor handed the man the small brown bottle, which contained a mercury solution. With that, the solder pulled his pants up and left the room.

"Okay, call in the next man," the doctor ordered. There was a steady stream of soldiers in and out of the office until the last of the soldiers was seen. The parade of boils, cuts, and minor ailments of the soldiers filled the day.

Once all of the soldiers had been tended to, the doctor turned to Cheveyo and said, "Now, please present the neophytes that have come to see me." There were far fewer neophytes to see Dr. Brown. One gaunt man with a slumping posture entered the room. "What is your complaint?" the doctor asked. The man took off his shirt and exposed a back shredded of skin and oozing pus. Adjusting his spectacles on his nose, the doctor leaned in to get a closer look at the man's back. "This is the worst infection from a flogging I have seen yet," the doctor said, shaking his head. "I have been going to every Mission and I have protested at each one, but still the whippings continue."

The doctor held out his hand to Cheveyo, who learned to know what instruments the doctor required. Cheveyo handed the doctor a jar of bear oil. He scooped up a generous amount and began gently spreading it on the wincing neophyte's back. The soothing oil began to work on the man's slashed back, and the man began to relax. Cheveyo, having done this before, knew to grab a roll of cut up cloth. The doctor wrapped the neophyte's back in it. When he was done, he gave instructions to him through Cheveyo's interpretations. This went on for the rest of the day.

The next morning at breakfast, Cheveyo watched as Domona and Luna walked through the courtyard. He was approached by the alcalde. "You have proven yourself a fine worker, Cheveyo, and I know that you have been waiting to get an apartment with your woman and child. I will speak on your behalf to His Grace and get you an appointment for the marriage ceremony so you can be with your family. Cheveyo had been waiting for this news for a long time. Finally he would be with Domona.

Several weeks passed, and Cheveyo had not heard any more, until one day a soldier came up to him in the stables where he was working.

"Come with me," the soldier ordered.

Cheveyo, not knowing where he was being led, was a little worried as he followed the soldier toward the main chapel where the padre's office was.

"Wait here," the soldier stated. He turned and walked into the office. It seemed like forever to Cheveyo as he stood in the yard watching the hustle and bustle of the daily life at the Mission.

Finally, the soldier returned and said, "His Grace is too busy to see you. Now go, get back to work."

Cheveyo, disappointed and dejected, sulked back to the stables.

BRUNO

Bruno was walking to his quarters to sneak in a nap. He was tired from his journey to Monterey for a much-needed two days of rest and relaxation. He had spent his two nights there having the time of his life, drinking and lying in the arms of a plump woman. Yes, he had to pay to lie with her, but he felt it was well worth it.

As he walked past the clinic, the doctor summoned him. "Bruno, may I have a few words with you?"

"Of course, Doctor, what is it?" Bruno asked as he walked into the clinic.

"I will be going south to the Mission by the sea. It seems they are having an epidemic of consumption and fevers of unknown origin. I will need assistance. My assistant here—he pointed to Cheveyo—would be a good choice, as he has worked with me and knows my needs. How do I get permission to take him for a week or two?"

"I have the authority to grant your request. You may take him. When are you leaving so I can have the horses and cart ready?"

"We will leave in the morning," the doctor replied.

The next morning, Cheveyo was at the clinic early and very excited to go on this journey. He had only been out of the Mission a few times, to drive the carts full of hides and tallow to the harbor.

The cart was set up with supplies, and the horses were ready to go when he arrived. The doctor appeared and got into the waiting cart. Cheveyo snapped the reigns and they were off.

Bruno watched with interest as they drove out of the Mission. "With Cheveyo gone, that means his woman is here alone. This is my chance to court her," Bruno said under his breath.

Cheveyo and Dr. Brown set out toward the south before the sun came up the next morning. Cheveyo drove the doctor's cart, and a neophyte named Gabriel accompanied them, driving a cart filled with supplies and goods for trade. A man named Francisco drove a third, empty cart to fill with supplies to bring back.

The road was dusty. It consisted of the fine sand that made up most of Alta California. The sand road was anywhere from an inch to a few inches thick, so Cheveyo had to take care to stay on the main trail so as not to bog down in it.

The ride was uneventful, and by the late afternoon the road became lined with trees. The fields were full of the soon to be harvested grains that grew here.

They rode past by huge herds of sheep and cattle. Then they crossed the Guadalupe River, the source of the water supply for this vast Mission. The Mission was called Santa Clara de Asisi, and it was the first of many Missions they were about to visit.

They passed by the remains of a building with evidence of a fire that left it all but destroyed. Moving along the entrance to the quadrangle, they saw a large chapel with four bells atop it and the offices, guest quarters, and church in a rectangular setting.

A neophyte greeted them as they entered the compound. He took hold of the reins and directed the doctor to his quarters. He then took the horses to the stable and showed Cheveyo and the others to the adobe lodge where the neophytes stayed.

A bell rang every evening at sundown while they were there, as it had since the day it had been erected.

Tired from his journey, Cheveyo went to his sleeping mat directly after the evening meal.

The next day was busy with the usual helping Dr. Brown in the clinic. At the end of the long line of ailments that the doctor tended to there was some time to look around the compound. Cheveyo was interested in seeing how the neophytes got along here and if it was any different from his home Mission.

An outbreak of smallpox at this Mission prior to their arrival had taken many of the neophytes' lives as well as many soldiers.

Cheveyo was shown the burial ground that was still being dug. He had never seen so many bodies at one time. Men, women, and children were piled in a heap in different stages of decay. He had seen much death before but not like this. The bodies were decaying in the hot sun, every one of them covered in blisters. Some were oozing and some had blood dripping from them. He could scarcely bear to look at them without feeling bile rise up in his throat. The sight of those bodies haunted his sleep that night. He was glad when Dr. Brown was ready to move on the next morning.

Domona walked Luna to the children's quarters, as they were separate from the women's. The air was cool and the night sky so clear that many stars were lighting her way. She walked past the stables, a route that she seldom took because it took longer to reach the women's lodge, but the fresh air felt so good.

All at once, an arm grabbed around her neck and a hand clasped over her mouth. She ripped at the hairy arm with her nails, trying to pull it away from her face to no avail. She was being dragged into the stable. She was thrown down onto a bed of straw with the weight of the man on top of her.

She could not fathom what was taking place—it was happening so fast. Shocking reality hit her as a cold chill came over the front of her and she heard the ripping of her tunic that exposed her body. A hand began stroking her breasts. Tears starting to form now, she tried to kick, but the weight of this beast was upon her. Her hands were being restrained at the wrists, held fast above her head against the straw where she lay. His other hand was over her mouth. She fought so desperately, but his body was holding her down. She could barely breathe from the weight of it. She closed her legs tight but could feel a knee wedge between her thighs with such force that it pinched her skin. The hand over her mouth released only to be replaced by a mouth over hers. She heard the rustling of the man's panta-loons and braced for what was next.

As her attacker's free hand fumbled with his trouser closure, she could feel a sudden hot pain between her legs. She gave a wince as he penetrated her. Unable to fight this monster on top of her, she gave in. Thrust after thrust...she just wanted this to end. His slobbering drool mixed with the tears rolling down her face. He whispered, "I love you, I love you."

A few more thrusts and then he shuddered and lay still. His heavy breathing disgusted her until she felt she might vomit. He stood up and adjusted his pantaloons as he stumbled toward the barn door. He was in the shadows, so she could not identify the man. Then he was gone.

She lay there not moving for a moment. Tears streaming down her face, she sat up and gathered the remains of her tattered tunic. Recovering her composure as best she could, she stood up. "I have to go to the women's quarters before final count. I don't want it known what just happened here." She gathered her torn tunic and wiped her face. She crept to the door of the stable and looked out. Seeing no one, she limped her way back to the women's dorm and went to her bed, feeling ashamed and dishonored.

Cheveyo, Dr. Brown, and the rest of their party left Mission Asisi early the next morning after eating a meal of fresh fruits from the garden, baked bread, and fresh meat that had been slaughtered for the occasion. The sky was free of clouds, and it was already warm. Even with the sun just peeking over the horizon, he could tell it was going to be a hot day.

The scenery took Cheveyo's mind off of the horror of the way the people had died and what their bodies looked like covered in blisters, even on the faces, that he had witnessed at the Mission of Santa Clara. There were fewer and fewer cattle to see as they left the land surrounding the Mission. Soon they saw none, and the beauty of the land was all he could see.

He had to navigate the cart carefully on the dusty trail. The edges of it had thicker sand, and it was easy for the wheels of the cart to bog down. This part of the valley was surrounded by a chain of rugged mountains with steep hills dotted with dark patches of chaparral at the top.

In the distance, he could see that they would be heading up an incline. The trail was steep in some spots and then flattened out. As they got higher up the mountain slope, Cheveyo had to maneuver around rocks at the edge of the trail that had broken off of the hillside. The rocks were small at first, and then they became larger as they climbed up the hill. Some of the rocks were as large as the cart, and much care had to be taken to get around them. Around the next bend, they were stopped in the tracks by a huge boulder blocking the road.

Cheveyo stopped and got off the cart to examine the blockage of the road from the boulder. He directed Dr. Brown to get out of the cart and walk to the side of the road just past the boulder. The doctor grabbed his medical bag with his tools and carefully walked past the boulder.

There was just enough room to pass two wheels of the cart on the road and two wheels hanging off the edge. Guiding the horse, who bucked and stammered at the unbalance of the cart, he walked in front of the horse and pulled the reins. The cart was now free of the blockage. Cheveyo pulled it forward and, handing the reins to Dr. Brown, walked past the boulder to the second cart in their entourage.

Grabbing the reins of the horse that was hitched to the second cart, Cheveyo instructed Gabriel to walk to the end of the cart and push it. He hoped this would not burden the horse as it had the first one.

Again, the cart's two wheels hung over the edge of the road, and again the horse struggled to pull the tilted cart. This cart was full of supplies and trade goods, so it was harder to get this cart around the boulder. With Cheveyo pulling in front and Gabriel pushing in the rear, they got the cart through the blockage. He handed the reins to Dr. Brown.

As he turned to approach the third cart, which he knew should be easier since it was empty, Cheveyo observed that the driver of the third cart, Francisco, had already started to proceed past the boulder with the two right wheels hanging over the edge. The horse did not like this and started to protest, its hind legs bucking and its front legs flailing violently. Cheveyo tried to grab the reins, but he could not. The horse's kicking legs prevented him from doing so. The horse began to walk in reverse, and this caused both back wheels of the cart to go off the edge. Francisco jumped behind the cart to push it back up on the road. The horse, still backing up, pushed the whole cart off the edge. Francisco, hanging on the cart, was jolted out and left dangling on the back of the cart. The horse at the front of all this was being pulled backward by the dangling cart. Francisco was kicking and screaming and the cart was fully over the edge of the road.

Thinking quickly, Cheveyo ran to his cart and took the reins from Dr. Brown's hands. Pulling his horse to the horse that was now whining from fright, he tied the reins from one horse to the other and had his horse back up, cart and all.

At first, nothing was happening—it was a standoff. Then, slowly, as Cheveyo gave commands to his horse and pushed at the horse to back up, the third cart horse jumped in line and walked slowly forward. The cart creaked and groaned and sounded as if it would break apart, but finally the two front wheels on solid ground were followed by the two back wheels on solid ground and finally a frightened Francisco. "Ay ca rumba!" Francisco cried as he made the sign of the Holy cross with his hand on his body and kissed to the sky. "You saved my hide, Amigo!" said Francisco.

With all the carts back on the road and everyone all in one piece, they set off on the decline of the mountain.

By day's end, the descent down the mountain was complete. They continued down the road to the Mission of San Juan Batista.

The road leveled out, and it was a smooth ride the rest of the way. The sun was getting low in the western sky, and it would soon be dark. Dr. Brown insisted on Cheveyo riding a little faster to get to Mission San Juan Batista before it got too dark.

Cheveyo could see that there were fresh bear tracks on this road—many of them. That made the doctor a little nervous as he pointed out that there were bear all around this territory.

Cheveyo heard a rustling in the bushes just ahead of the road. He stopped the cart and put his hand up for silence. The bushes began to quake and tremble and out jumped a buck with antlers as wide as any he'd seen along with a few does with babies in tow. Cheveyo gave a sigh of relief as they continued along the road.

The usual signs that they were nearing the entrance to the Mission were becoming apparent. The fields were full of planted corn and beans of several varieties. There was even a vast vineyard with ripe grapes hanging on the vine. The vine leaves happily danced in the breeze. Beyond this, a beautiful garden lined the pathway to the two-story adobe building painted pristine white with a red-tiled roof and a bell tower. Continuing on, they rode past a long row of massive columns that was the pathway to the other parts of the Mission.

They were greeted by a neophyte who took the reins and led the horse-drawn cart to the church. He instructed Dr. Brown to disembark and told him he would show him to his quarters. Cheveyo and Francisco waited with the carts. Gabriel left the group, as he would be staying here permanently. The neophyte returned and led the two carts and riders to the stables, where he instructed them to put up the horses and then pointed to where they would be staying. He also informed them that the bell would toll for the evening meal and not to miss it if they wanted to eat.

Cheveyo put up his horse and walked over to the quarters of the neophytes. It was under construction, so it still had only one wall. The wall was made of adobe and was four feet thick. The roof was made of tules tied together with strips of leather. Taking the blanket someone handed to him, Cheveyo found an empty spot and lay his tired body on top of the blanket.

When he woke to the sound of the evening bell, he did not remember falling asleep...he had been so tired. Shaking the sleep from his groggy head, he debated with himself as to how great his hunger was compared to his fatigue. His hunger won, and he got up and proceeded to the line of neophytes awaiting their turn at getting food. A mixture of beans green in color, corn, and some meat in a mush was served. To Cheveyo it was the best meal he had eaten in a long time.

After the evening meal, he walked around to speak to groups of neophytes to learn information on where they were from, how they had come to be here, and how they were faring.

He learned that the people were of the coastal tribes and were a peaceful and trusting people before they were captured and their village destroyed. That they were expected to learn the ways of the padres, and when they did not learn fast enough or did not do their lessons properly, they were whipped. The ones who attempted to escape were recaptured and whipped and put in shackles, sometimes for many days. Many had died from the overworking, starving, and sickness that they were forced to endure.

This opened his eyes to the realization that it was not just his people whom this had happened to; it had happened to all the people of the local tribes. After Cheveyo heard many neophytes tell their stories, the bell rang to signal retiring for the day. He went back to his sleeping blanket with too much on his mind to sleep.

The next morning, Cheveyo, a little sleepy form lack of sleep, found the clinic and spent the day helping Dr. Brown with an assortment of ailments—first the soldiers, then the neophytes.

One of the young men came in with a cloth tied around his hand that he was supporting with his other hand. Cheveyo leaned in to see what was under the cloth wrapping. The doctor unwrapped the man's hand, and Cheveyo grimaced at what he saw. "I was bitten by the koking-wungwa," the young man said.

The doctor looked at Cheveyo with a puzzled look on his face and said, "Translate, please."

"He has been bitten by the spider you know as a tarantula," Cheveyo said.

Dr. Brown nodded his head in agreement and took the young man's hand. Turning it over and back and examining the young man's eyes and mouth, he determined that this young man was probably allergic to the venom of the spider.

The man's hand had swelled to twice its normal size and had turned a purplish hue. The bite site was bright red. First, Dr. Brown cleaned the site, and then he put some salve on it. "You will be all right. I don't know of anyone who has died from the bite of a tarantula. You will be in discomfort for a few days, however. I will give you some elixir to drink, which will help with the pain."

Finishing up with the line of patients with the usual complaints, Cheveyo noticed the faces of the people, the neophytes, all had a ghostlike appearance—their skin was gray, and they looked thin and gaunt, with lifeless expressions on their faces.

Thinking to himself that these people had been living in the Missions longer than he had, he wondered, *Is this what is to become of me?*

Just then, the evening meal bell rang. Their stay here seemed like an eternity to him. Finally the doctor announced that he was ready to move on to the next Mission.

They left early in morning before sunrise. Dr. Brown, Cheveyo, and Francisco arrived at the Presidio at Monterey by midmorning and were immediately taken to the clinic. It was a large room with white adobe walls; cots lined the room and there were narrow walkways between them. On many cots were soldiers with a variety of wounds and illnesses. Bloodied bandages littered the floor.

Dr. Brown was led to the center of the room, where a man in a blood-soaked apron stood. He looked at Dr. Brown as he sewed a gash on a soldier. "Finally, a real doctor," the man said.

Dr. Brown rolled up his sleeves and dipped his hands in a bucket of water. Turning to the slab, he said, "What have we here?"

On the slab was a young soldier whose gut was torn open by a knife. The doctor shook his head as he examined the wound. "Cheveyo take, this man to a cot and make sure he is made comfortable." Turning to the man, Dr. Brown lifted his head and had him drink from a little brown bottle. Cheveyo understood the meaning, as he had been working so closely with the doctor for months. He knew there was nothing he could do for the soldier.

They worked well into the night until finally Dr. Brown told a soldier, "Take my helper here and give him food and a place to sleep tonight."

The soldier, nodding his head, led Cheveyo to an area behind the grand walls of the Presidio. There he pointed to a long structure made of tules. "Neophytes stay here," he said. The soldier turned and left Cheveyo standing at the entrance.

Cheveyo entered the lodge, found a place, and recognized Francisco.

"Did you eat?" Francisco asked Cheveyo.

"No, I was helping the doctor from the moment we got here. My gut is speaking loudly and demanding food," Cheveyo said, rubbing his stomach.

Francisco reached under his blanket and pulled out a piece of meat that he had saved from the evening meal. "Here, take this—I was saving it to eat in the night, but you need it more than I."

As he ate, Francisco talked. "I have heard that Spain, where the padre's home is, is no longer in charge of this land and that it now belongs to Mexico. I found out that San Juan from our Mission has led a revolt against the Mission here and the soldiers from here have been fighting with him. They say that many of San Juan's followers have been killed. The battle of the revolt of the neophytes against the soldiers has been a deadly one." Cheveyo listened as Francisco gave him all the information he had gathered from other neophytes who lived at this Presidio in Monterey. Cheveyo devoured the meat. He lay down and fell fast asleep.

The days were endless with the tending of the wounds of the soldiers. Many nights, after a long day helping Dr. Brown in the clinic, he would go back to the neophytes' lodge and lie on his blanket with thoughts of Domona. How their lives would be better upon his return to the Mission. He would have the marriage ceremony and get them an apartment when he returned so they could be together once again and be a family. He would ask the doctor for his assistance in getting this for him.

When at last they left this Mission, they headed northwest, turning onto a road that followed a canyon between the high mountains that ran along the coast. The thick blanket of fog was refreshing to Cheveyo. It covered the whole scene so that the road ahead was a mystery.

The road was not as sandy here, and the cart wheels did not bog down as much. As the day unfolded, the fog began to lift, shedding light on the beautiful scenery of the mountains all around.

The twists and turns in the road took them through a canyon that was lined with trees that were taller than any Cheveyo had ever imagined.

The fog lifted, and the warm sun felt good on Cheveyo's face. He looked up to see a few clouds in the sky—floating shapes of images that occupied his mind as he drove the cart down the road. The land was nothing but sagebrushes and a few tall trees and the steep hillside of the mountain that surrounded them.

After traveling about four leagues, they heard the voices of some men yelling and a gunshot rang out. A man screamed, and there was ferocious growling the likes of which Cheveyo had never heard. As they drove around a bend in the road, they came upon a frightening scene.

A grizzly bear was atop a man. The man was screaming, and there were three other men at a distance, jumping and hollering at the bear. But the bear was not deterred and continued to maul his victim.

Cheveyo, observing the situation, jumped into action. He instructed the doctor to get down from the cart and to remain at a safe distance from the grizzly scene. Cheveyo then jumped onto the horse that pulled the cart, kicked the sides of the horse, and charged at the bear. The horse, reacting to the kick, galloped full steam at the bear.

The bear stood up on his hind legs, waving his paws toward the horse. The horse became frightened, but at Cheveyo's command it bucked up on its hind legs, flailing its front hooves. The horse's hooves struck the bear several time, and the bear swung at the horse, its razor sharp claws coming within inches of Cheveyo's face. The horse whinnied and struck the bear full in the face with its front hooves. That was enough for the bear. Bloodied from the blow to its face and the blood from the victim, the bear turned and ran away.

Dr. Brown grabbed his medical bag. He and everyone who was there ran to the badly injured victim. The injured man was still alive but barely moving. Cheveyo looked around at the men. He could see that they were vaqueros. He could also see that the one who had been mauled by the bear was in bad shape.

The injured man had half of his scalp ripped off; it was a dangling flap of hairy and bloody skin. Upon further examination, they could see that the front of the man's thigh was completely gone. A gaping hole was now where muscle and flesh used to be. The man was unconscious. Cheveyo stood over the man, stunned at the sight.

The doctor began barking orders. "Where are you staying? Put this man in the back of the empty cart. I need to get him to a clean dry area. He needs stitching to stop that bleeding or he will die from loss of blood."

The vaqueros did as instructed, placing their injured companion in the empty cart and pointing in the direction just beyond the hill. Cheveyo drove the cart as Dr. Brown in the cart tended to the injured man.

They arrived at a small adobe building that appeared to be the only building around this desolate area. Two of the vaqueros grabbed their injured friend, and the other ran ahead to open the door and ready a cot.

Cheveyo stayed outside, as there was not much room in the tiny building and he was a little shaken at the damage that a bear was capable of doing. He had never seen anything like it.

After a while, Dr. Brown came out, wiping his hands. "I've done all that I can for the poor soul. It is in God's hands now."

They headed to the next Mission, San Carlos Borromeo de Carmelo.

They arrived at the Mission after the evening meal and were greeted by neophytes, who directed Dr. Brown to his quarters and told him that he would bring some cheese, bread and wine to his quarters. Cheveyo could feel his stomach grumble at the mention of food. He hadn't eaten anything since early morning. The memory of the mangled leg of the vaquero by the bear was still fresh in his mind, so he just focused on how tired he was. It was late, and he was so tired he curled up in the back of the cart to sleep. He would make up for not eating tonight at the morning meal the next day.

Morning came all too fast. He heard the meal bell ring and jumped up, not wanting to miss this meal. He was pleasantly surprised to see that there was beef and bread served to neophytes at this Mission. The surplus of meat was the result of too many head of cattle, and he learned that fifty head a month had to be slaughtered on a regular basis to keep the herd from becoming too large. This Mission also fed the Presidio at Monterey and had heads of cattle in the thousands. The production of hides and tallow was big business here. The Missions then shipped these to the Americas.

He also learned that this was the Mission where the founding father of all Missions was buried. This Mission was the headquarters and the hub of all the Missions. It was a very busy place.

Dr. Brown informed Cheveyo that they would be leaving right away to go to the Mission at Santa Cruz, a short distance away. There was no room to stay here, since there were many dignitaries and heads of state from Mexico visiting at this particular time. Before he left, Dr. Brown asked the padre and his associates for a meeting.

Dr. Brown spoke with concern. "Your Grace, Gentlemen, I have noticed an epidemic of the syphilis here among your men."

"Alas," said the padre, "we do everything we can to keep the soldiers in line. But since the change of control from Spain, we take what we can get from what we are offered for our soldiering. The gambling, the drinking, the fornications are all part of the life of a soldier, I'm afraid."

"Humph!" said Dr. Brown in disgust. "Well, I can't treat them all. I would need a sea of mercury to do that!" With that, the doctor turned to leave. "Good day, Your Grace, gentlemen."

The doctor climbed into the cart next to Cheveyo, and the caravan proceeded on its way. Leading the two carts, Cheveyo drove to the Santa Cruz Mission. They set out on the road in a northerly direction. At first the road took them over rolling hills, then high hills, and then through a canyon lined with the most beautiful trees that Cheveyo had ever seen. The bases of these trees were very large.

The road was easy for the cattle and horses and the caballeros that tend them. They traveled up an incline lined with these trees that became a thick forest of lush redwoods.

They reached the summit and took in the beauty of the coastline below. The waves crashing onto the shore from this height were breathtaking. The sun was high in the cloudless sky, and a cool breeze whipped through Cheveyo's hair. On the other side of the summit was a green canyon of shrubs and chaparral. The sharp peak of the mountain on the other side of the canyon stretched out for miles as far as he could see.

"We must be at the top of the world," he said under his breath.

On their descent down the mountain, they were accompanied by a bunch of deer flitting through the brush. These were fine roads that wound up valleys, through and across canyons, over ridges, and finally along steep hillsides of golden wild wheat waving in the wind.

Soon they came upon a Mission that sat near a clear stream. Neat trees lined the path to the Mission. Here there was an adobe church and a wooden building next to it with several buildings forming the typical quad.

This Mission was the smallest that Cheveyo had seen, but the usual hustle and bustle of Mission life abounded. Rich fields of corn and beans and a healthy vineyard surrounded the Santa Cruz Mission with thousands of head of cattle dotting the countryside.

Stopping at the church, Dr. Brown went to the chapel to inquire about his quarters and check in with the padre.

Cheveyo found the neophytes' quarters and settled in. He noticed that there was only a handful of neophytes at this Mission. After the evening meal, he learned that there had been an uprising many years before and the neophytes had killed the padre. The Mission had had floods and a mass exodus by the neophytes. The work load was unbearable. The demand for the cowhides kept them working at a deadly pace.

The stay here was the hardest and the longest.

They set out again, heading north up the coast road. Their destination was the San Francisco Presidio. The day started out sunny and cool. As they made their way up the coast, the fog set in. Soon they were blanketed by a thick, dense fog. The road was dry and sandy, with sagebrush dotted along the way. Before long, Cheveyo's hair hung wet and clung to his face from the dampness of the fog.

By afternoon, they reached a large field of wheat marking the boundary of the San Francisco Presidio. It was a small place in comparison to his home Mission.

He witnessed neophytes that were busy bringing food from the fields to the kitchen where it was cooked to feed the soldiers. This Presidio was independent and did not get any help from the Mission south of it.

The Presidio was situated on the gateway to the Bay at San Francisco. It was cold and damp. Each gust of wind sent a chill Cheveyo felt down to his bones. The cold made him miss his Mission; he longed to get back and be warm next to Domona.

The parade of soldiers at the clinic began with the usual complaints. Then came the neophytes, as the days wore on. Cheveyo settled into a small adobe building that housed the neophytes, and just as he was going to sleep one night, the bed began to jiggle; at first it was light, and then the shaking grew more intense. He jumped to his feet as the small room started to sway and the whole ground under his feet shook violently, sending him careening to the ground.

"EARTHQUAKE!" someone shouted.

Cheveyo was knocked off his feet, and he fell to the earth on his knees. He scrambled toward the door as pieces of adobe fell like rain all around him. At first it was small pieces, and then large chunks of adobe began to fall, some hitting him on the head.

Making it to the doorway, he rolled out the door in a summersault just as the building collapsed. That was when he noticed that the shaking had stopped and that everyone was standing outside in the courtyard. Dust hung thick in the air and everywhere buildings had fallen in upon themselves.

Looking around, Cheveyo noticed neophyte women crying and a soldier with streaks of blood running down his face from a cut on his forehead. Dozens were walking around in a daze, afraid to go back inside. Soldiers were running around to collapsed buildings in an attempt to pull out victims who were trapped under rubble.

Cheveyo rounded up a group of neophytes and led them to the worst of the collapsed buildings. Faint voices could be heard under the debris. He ran to the ruins, lifting large chunks of the adobe. At last, soldiers came to help, and the last large piece of adobe was lifted. There were three bodies of neophytes, two dead and one barely alive.

The injured were taken to an outside clinic in the center of the courtyard for Dr. Brown to attend to. The dead neophytes and soldiers alike, crushed and bloodied, were placed in a cart to take to the burial grounds.

Just then, an aftershock hit and the panic started all over again. Screams could be heard as people ran for safety only to find none.

Nobody slept that night. A cold and damp fog greeted them the next day. The extent of the damage was reviewed—it was extensive. The buildings that were still standing were too unstable to enter. Food was prepared out of doors, although not many could eat, their shock was so great.

Still shaken by the earthquake, Cheveyo was very anxious to leave the Presidio, get as far away from there as possible, and return to Domona. His thoughts of her occupied his mind more than ever. They took the road to the beach, leaving behind the carts and horses. The group boarded a rowboat that took them to a ship in the bay. Cheveyo had never been on a ship of any kind before, especially one of this size.

They set sail on the short trip across the San Francisco Bay. The sailors were well seasoned and went about their tasks efficiently. Still, the ship pitched and bounced with the motion of the waves and the wind punching it along.

The ship landed on the north shore and they were greeted by a soldier with horses. They mounted the horses and rode the rest of the way to San Rafael Archangel, the next Mission on their journey.

The trail to the Mission was up a steep incline surrounded by sage and brush. The horse's steps were strong and true, and soon they reached the top of the hill overlooking the Bay below. Cheveyo looked around and was astonished by the beauty of the scenery. The high hills, the Bay below, the San Francisco peninsula jutting out into the green-blue water.

They arrived at the chapel but did not stop there. Next to the chapel was a new adobe building that used for a hospital. This was designed to treat neophytes that became ill. They immediately got to work.

The days wore on, and at the end of one work day Dr. Brown turned to Cheveyo and said, "Son, I am staying on here. I need to study new techniques, and here is where I will learn them. You have been a great help to me these last few months. Tomorrow, you will go home. I have sent a letter ahead making all the arrangements. There is just one last thing." Dr. Brown handed him a letter. "Please give this to His Grace when you get back to your home Mission." Cheveyo took the letter and tucked it into his waistband.

After he finished cleaning, he gathered his belongings, including the new things he had gotten along his journey—beautiful shells for a necklace for Domona and a doll made of grass for Luna. His heart was filled with joy; he was finally going home.

The sun woke Cheveyo up the next morning. He was eager to start his trek back home. After saying good-bye to Dr. Brown, he was escorted to the shore. Just past the wave break, a tule canoe was waiting for him. Wading out to it in waist-deep water, he climbed aboard.

The tule canoe was fifteen feet long, paddled by two neophytes. The canoe was as sturdy as any Cheveyo had seen. He had seen smaller ones being built at his village in his youth. He remembered how it took three days to build once the tules were laid out to half dry in the sun. Then the tules were tied together in bundles with a willow branch in the middle for strength. The bottom tule was the longest. Next, the shorter bundles were tied to the bottom bundle until the sides were built. The ends were tied together tightly to make it waterproof. Then branches were cut and shaped for paddles.

They set out in the coolness of the morning when the water was at its calmest. The men paddling the canoe were quite proficient, and soon they were traveling at a great speed.

About midday, the water became choppy. The rolling of the sea made the canoe rise ten feet high and then smash back down. Cheveyo, hoping that he was hiding his fear that he would be thrown out into the choppy water, held tightly onto the side of the canoe. He could swim but was not a strong swimmer. By the after-noon, the water became calm again.

Cheveyo sat back and thought about Domona, how he had missed her and how much Luna must have grown. This trip with Dr. Brown that he had thought was going to be short had turned into six months away from her.

"There is the shore!" said the oarsman.

Cheveyo could see the shore in the distance. As they ap-proached it, he could see that there were three riders on horse-back and several other rider less horses. Not until the canoe was sliding onto the beach could he see that it was Bruno sitting atop a horse. Bruno had a condescending smirk on his face.

"Welcome home," Bruno said with distain as he handed Cheveyo the reins of a horse.

The group rode well into the night. With Bruno riding behind him, he could feel the man's piercing eyes on him the whole way back. Upon his return, he handed the letter that Dr. Brown had given him to the alcalde with instructions to give to the padre. Arriving back at his Mission, San Jose, Cheveyo realized how much he loved his little family and would work on getting the marriage done so they could get an apartment.

The Mission apartments for the married couples were in a sec-tion of the Mission behind the compound. The neophytes that lived here worked at the Mission.

Cheveyo wasted no time before sneaking to the women's dor-mitory. He called up to the window with iron bars on it. This was a window in a second floor landing whereby the women were court-ed by perspective marriage partners. Cheveyo called up to the win-dow. A young neophyte woman came to the window.

"Please get Domona—I have returned and I must see her," Cheveyo shouted.

The young woman left, and a few minutes later Domona appeared at the window.

"Dom, I'm back—oh, how I have missed you, my love," Cheveyo crooned.

"Cheveyo, my love," Domona said as tears streamed down her face. "I am so happy to see you home safe."

"I will work on getting the ceremony so we can have an apartment. So we can be together as a family!"

"Hey, you!" a voice bellowed out. Cheveyo turned toward the sound. It was a soldier who was guarding the doorway to the women's quarters coming toward him at a fast pace. "Get away from there!"

Cheveyo called up to Domona, "I'll see you soon, my love," as he ran away.

Back at the stable the next day, Cheveyo went right back to work as he had done before his travels with Dr. Brown. He was mucking out the stable when he was approached by Bruno. "Come with me. His Grace requests your presence."

Bruno led him to the office of the padre. "Wait here," Bruno said, pointing to the ground they stood on. In a few minutes, the padre stepped out of the building into the warm sun.

"Ah, it is a lovely day. Cheveyo, my child, you have proven to be a faithful servant to the Mission and to Dr. Brown. I received a letter from him, and he had nothing but praises for you. He spoke of your desire to live in Holy matrimony with one of my neophyte daughters and live in the married apartments."

Cheveyo bowed his head and, holding his straw hat in his hands, answered, "Yes, Your Grace, more than anything."

"It is granted, my son. I will hold a ceremony tomorrow afternoon. Come to the chapel before the evening meal," the padre answered.

He could not believe what he had just heard. He had waited for so long. The letter that Dr. Brown had given to him that he had in turn given to Bruno contained a request to expedite his marriage. His heart filled with joy. "Thank you, Your Grace. We will see you in the chapel after services."

Bruno, standing next to the padre, had to hide the feelings of jealousy that welled up inside of him.

Cheveyo bowed to the padre and turned to find Domona. He wanted to tell her the good news—that they would finally be a family living together.

Cheveyo ran to the building that housed the materials to weave clothing, where Domona worked. There she was, sitting on a stool in front of a loom.

"Dom, I have great news—we are to be married tomorrow and will get our apartment!" Cheveyo said.

Domona's face lit up with joy at the news. "Oh, Cheveyo, we will be a family again."

Returning to the stable, Cheveyo got busy finishing his tasks for the day. Then a young neophyte rushed in and said, "Cheveyo, is the new doctor here? I need his services right away!"

A new doctor had been making rounds to all the missions once a month.

Cheveyo looked at the anxious youth, "No, he had to go the Mission hospital up north where Dr. Brown is, to learn of the newest medical procedures. He will not be back for a while."

The young neophyte looked defeated but said, "You have worked with the doctor, you must have some knowledge of illness. Please come and help my brother."

"What is wrong with him?" Cheveyo asked.

The youth led Cheveyo to the men's lodge, to a mat where a neophyte lay. Cheveyo removed the blanket from the sick man. The man lay still, very weak and near death. His limbs were swollen, and his face was so swollen he could not talk.

"His legs have swelled so that he is unable to walk, and he is in terrible pain. His gums in his mouth are bleeding and so swollen that he is unable to eat. I fear he will die soon unless you can save him. Please, you must help him," pleaded the youth.

Cheveyo looked at the young neophyte. "What food has he been eating?"

"The food has become less and less here. You have been away, and we are no longer fed the beans or corn or potatoes that we once had—only the soldiers get those now. There are no longer supplies coming from the ships. We have to live on what we have here and there is only cattle and horses, some onions, and a few potatoes. Will he die?"

Cheveyo had seen this before. He had seen these symptoms many times in his travels with Dr. Brown in the soldiers that had been to sea for many months without proper vegetables. "Go to the garden and find me one potato and one onion. If we act quickly, he will not die," Cheveyo instructed.

"I cannot. If I get caught stealing from the garden, I will be punished," the youth cried.

"It is the only way to heal your brother. He needs the nourishment that only those items can provide. Now go!" Cheveyo pointed toward the garden.

The young neophyte ran off to the garden. Cheveyo looked more closely at the ill man. He confirmed in his mind what he had suspected. The ill man's legs were swollen to twice their size. Cheveyo pressed on the skin and it stayed indented—no elasticity. Next he looked into the man's mouth. The gums were so swollen he could not see the back of his throat, and some of the man's teeth had fallen out.

Cheveyo looked the ill man in the eyes. "You are a native brother, and I will do what I can to help you survive."

The young neophyte returned with a small potato and an onion that was a little overripe as instructed. Cheveyo took them and got his knife that he had brought from the stable. He cut the potato and onion into small pieces. With a clay vessel, he mashed the mixture up into a mush, adding water to it. It made a soup-like tonic. He held up the ill man's head and gently poured some of the mixture into his mouth. The ill man winced in pain and moaned in agony as the juice coated his sore lips and gums and then his swollen throat.

Cheveyo looked at the youth. "Your brother has what is known as scurvy. It is caused from not eating the proper foods he needs to survive. You must do as I have just done, pouring the liquid into his mouth and throat throughout the day, and for the next few days. Until he is able to eat the rest of the mixture."

The youth thanked Cheveyo. "I will do just as I have seen you do. Thank you for saving my brother. You are a true shaman."

Cheveyo went back to the stable to finish his day's work.

The day of the marriage ceremony arrived. Cheveyo was too excited to sleep. He was to meet Domona at the chapel with other couples joining in marriage. He saw Domona walking into the chapel with Luna in tow. She had on a flowing tunic and, to Cheveyo, looked so beautiful.

The ceremony was performed by the padre. This was the first time Cheveyo was allowed to be close to Domona in a public setting. She had aged a little, from the harsh working conditions and poor diet or sickness, as had all those who came to this place—those from his village who were still alive. But to him she looked as beautiful as the first time he had seen her.

They walked hand in hand to the area behind the compound where there was an apartment available to them. They spent a good part of the remaining daylight putting down a fresh tule floor and bedding.

When it was time for the evening meal, they went as a family, and Cheveyo was beaming with pride. After the meal and before turning in for the night, he went to the men's lodge to visit the ill man who had scurvy. He saw a much-improved man. He was sitting up and eating acorn meal that had beans in it. The swelling of his legs had gone down.

"Thank you, Cheveyo. You saved me and are truly a shaman," said the man.

Cheveyo said, "I am happy that you are better." He took his leave.

Then he returned to his apartment, to his first night with Domona since the capture. It was dark in the little apartment, only the soft glow from the coals in a fire pit in the center of the hut. He found his way to where Domona lay quietly breathing. He reached for her and she sat up. He slid her tunic off and began to run his hands over her body and caressing her, kissing her mouth and neck and finally sucking the roundness of her breasts. He gently ran his hands over her full breasts down her sides to her belly. His hands stopped at her belly when he noticed that her belly was large with child. He grabbed her by her shoulders and pushed her away from himself. He looked down at her ample belly and then at her face in the glow of the embers.

He sat upright. "Domona, you are with child? How can this be? We have not been together in many, many months. Have you found another? Someone you love and want to be with? I don't understand," he cried.

She looked at him in the dim firelight and began to cry. At first it was just a few tears, and then she was hysterically sobbing. "Oh, Cheveyo," she struggled to say, "I was violated! The night you left, I was walking back from taking Luna to the children's quarters. I walked past the stables and was grabbed from behind. I never saw who it was. Cheveyo, I was raped." Tears now streaming down her cheeks, she put her hands over her face, reliving the shame she had felt that night. "I have not told anyone. I'm so ashamed and now I have this reminder, this baby—I hate it!" she said and punched herself in the belly.

Cheveyo pulled her to him and held her tightly. "I love you, my wife." That is all that he could manage to say with the rage that welled up inside of him so much so that it leaked out of his eyes in form of tears.

Cheveyo put his arms around his wife and held her close. He lay down with her head resting on his chest and held her gently until she fell asleep. Sleep eluded him the rest of the night. He was angry at himself. He blamed himself for leaving her alone and unprotected all these months and he was angry at whoever had defiled his wife.

The days rolled on, and Domona's belly continued to grow. Cheveyo kept busy at the stable, cleaning and taking care of the horses. Neophytes would come to him with various ailments, as if he were a doctor.

One day, a soldier came to him holding his jaw with his hand. He had a cloth tied around his head. "Can you fix my tooth?" the soldier asked.

Cheveyo looked at the man with contempt. To him, all soldiers were the one who had raped and impregnated his wife. To him this could be the man, so he decided he would make him pay. "No, I'm not a doctor," he told the soldier.

"But you worked with the doctor and surely you saw how he worked. Please, I am in so much pain; you must help me," the soldier begged.

Cheveyo looked at the soldier, took in a breath, and snorted out of his nose. "All right, come with me." He led the soldier to a wooden bench that ran along the wall. Moving a bucket and some rope out of the way, he pointed to the bench. "Sit here," he ordered.

The soldier sat on the bench, and Cheveyo reached for tool used to take nails out of the hooves of horses. It was rusty and caked with mud. Cheveyo wiped the mud off on his pantaloons. "Okay, open wide," he said.

The soldier opened his mouth, and Cheveyo could see that one of the back molars was black with decay. A vile stench emanated from the soldier's mouth. Taking a deep breath and holding it, he put his hand on the soldier's head and shoved it against the wall a little harder than necessary. Placing the pliers on the soldier's tooth, he pulled forward and backward slamming the soldier's head against the wall repeatedly. "Hmm, this is not going to work. Sit on the floor next to the bench," Cheveyo instructed.

The soldier complied, and Cheveyo stood over him, again putting his hand on the soldier's forehead. Again he pulled and tugged, purposely slamming the soldier's head against the wall all the while the soldier screamed in agony.

After a while, Cheveyo grew tired of this game and decided to put more effort into pulling out the tooth. Still standing over the soldier, he placed his foot on the soldier's shoulder to brace himself and, holding the pliers with both hands this time, he pulled as hard as he could as the soldier screamed like a woman out popped the blackened tooth with a bloody root. "There, you are cured," Cheveyo said as he released the pliers and the black tooth fell onto the round belly of the soldier. The soldier spit out some blood and stood up, rubbing his throbbing jaw. "Thank you. I do feel much better." He walked out the stable door.

Cheveyo followed the soldier to the door. Looking across the compound toward the Mission entrance, he saw Bruno ride in on horseback with several soldiers and recaptured runaways.

Domona had just stepped into the compound to go to the building where she worked. Bruno saw her and could not believe his eyes. "She is with child. She has my child. It can only be mine," he said in a whisper to himself. A smile came over his whole face. He counted the months in his head since the night he had taken her against her will in the barn. In his warped mind, it was the night that he had *made sweet love to her...*when Cheveyo had been gone with Dr. Brown. "I'm to be a father!" he whispered aloud with elation.

Cheveyo glared at Bruno from the stable entrance; all the soldiers here were now the suspected rapist. He did not trust any of them. He loathed them all, but especially Bruno. He did not like the way Bruno looked at his wife, the way he seemed to lust for her.

The weeks passed by. Domona was anxious for the birth, and Cheveyo wondered how he could love and raise this child. After all, in his village there had been many children who were orphaned and cared for by everyone, but this was different—this child had been conceived in an act of violence and was unwanted by him and his wife.

Back at their apartment after a long day, Cheveyo did not find Domona, but Luna was there alone. "Where is Mama?" he asked Luna.

"I don't know, Papa, she never came to get me after my lessons. I walked here by myself," Luna said.

Cheveyo began to look for his wife. He went to the women's dorm first, thinking she might have visited friends there. He shouted up to the porthole, "Hello—is Domona in there?"

A dark-haired young neophyte woman peered out of the porthole. "I have not seen her, but wait a moment and I will go ask the others if they saw her after her work day."

The young woman left the porthole and returned a short time later. "No one has seen her since the morning meal."

Cheveyo, not liking this news, began to worry. He began frantically running to each building searching for her. He asked other neophytes, men and women alike, if they had seen his wife. No one had.

He decided to go back to the apartment to see if she had returned. She had not. He sat and waited with Luna. Hours passed, and still no Domona. Cheveyo was sick with worry.

Just before daylight, after a long, sleepless night of worry, Domona came into the apartment. She was drenched in sweat and had dirt and blood on her hands and on the front of her tunic. She was out of breath.

"Domona, where have you been all night? I was so worried."

"Cheveyo, the baby came," she sighed.

"Oh, Domona, are you well? But where is the child?" he asked.

She sat down on her haunches, wringing her hands, took a deep breath, and told him the story.

"In the morning, I felt the pains of the birth coming on. I crept quietly to the edge of the cornfields, far from any buildings or people. I gathered up some of the stalks to make a bed for myself and waited for the birth. All night, the pains were getting stronger and stronger. When the time came for the birth, I squatted and pushed the baby out. There it lay in the dirt. It was a girl." Domona sighed and then continued. "I bit the cord to separate myself from this thing I hated. Setting the baby aside, I dug a hole in the ground, a deep hole. I picked her up with my dirt-covered hands, and the infant began to whimper. I placed the baby in the hole that I dug. The little baby lay there in the dirt hole with her little arms reaching for me, for the love a mother should have for her child...but there was none. I stared down at the little girl in the dirt hole for a moment. Looking around, I stood up as blood and fluid gushed down my leg and found a rock. I stumbled over to the rock. I was so weak, but I picked up the rock, the weight of it causing me to lose my balance, and I stumbled and fell to my knees. I went back to where the baby lay in the dirt hole. Still on my knees, I leaned over the baby. Mustering all my strength, I raised the rock high above my head. It teetered there briefly and then all my might and the weight of the rock came crashing down on the little head of the whimpering baby. The sound of crushing bone echoed in the still of the early morning. The baby girl lay still. I threw the rock aside, tissue clinging to the discarded rock. I scooped up handfuls of dirt and filled in the hole, burying the baby and my repulsion of the tiny thing along with it. Wiping my hands on my tunic, I crept in the shadows and made my way back to the apartment, making sure no one saw me." Domona looked at her husband and tears welled up in her eyes.

Cheveyo was relieved that his wife was safe, but he was also concerned. "Oh, Dom, what have you done? I would have been a father to the child. I fear the consequences of your actions."

"Cheveyo, the baby's eyes were all white. It was blind! The baby was blind!"

Cheveyo put his arms round Domona and cradled her as she wept hysterically.

Days passed, and they both thought their secret was safe until the still of a sleepy morning was broken by the bursting in of a soldier into their apartment. "What is this about?" the sleepy Cheveyo demanded as he sat up.

The soldier, followed by two more soldiers, grabbed Domona by the wrists, pulling her up from her sleeping mat. They dragged her outside. She was held by two soldiers and a third came up behind her and ripped open her tunic, exposing her bare back.

Cheveyo jumped up and ran out of the apartment with the intent of stopping the soldier's actions. He was met with a sword across his chest held by Bruno, stopping him in his tracks. Two more soldiers grabbed and held Cheveyo back while Bruno stepped up to Domona.

Bruno, now facing Domona, looked into her eyes. He knew what she had done with the baby...his baby. "Word gets around the compound about the lives of the people who live in it. I know you did something to the baby you carried inside you."

Domona stood defiantly. Bruno looked for some remorse but found none. He was especially saddened because it was his child that she had disposed of. He wanted an answer that could justify her actions. "Do you have anything to say?" he asked Domona, hoping she had a good one. She continued to stare silently straight ahead. Again he faced her with sadness in his eyes and asked, "Why did you kill the child?" She stood her ground and said nothing.

"Very well then, you have committed the sin of murder and will be punished by the whip," declared Bruno. He nodded to the soldier holding the whip.

Several lashes were struck onto the smooth brown back of Domona. The blood red streaks appeared immediately. Her cries for mercy fell on unsympathetic ears as did the pleading of Cheveyo to stop.

The soldiers holding Domona released her and she fell to her knees on the ground. A wooden log the size of a baby was thrown on the ground in front of her, and Bruno kicked it toward her. "You will carry this log as if it was your baby as further punishment until told not to."

Bruno, standing over her, bent down and shouted in her face, "That is for the killing of the baby!" He straightened up, spit at her, and then turned and walked away.

Cheveyo, released by the soldiers holding him, ran to her and gathered her up in his arms. She was in such pain. He carried her to the clinic, where he put bear oil on her back and gave her some liquid in a little brown bottle to ease the pain. He also gave her a sip of mercury, the only cure for syphilis. The soldier who had raped her must have infected her, Cheveyo surmised. In his time working with Dr. Brown, he had learned the symptoms. There were many soldiers at the Mission who had syphilis. Dr. Brown had told him that if a woman gives birth to a baby that is blinded, with only the whites of its eyes, this was probably caused by syphilis and would in all likelihood cause sterility in the woman, making it impossible to have future children.

He placed a blanket on the sedated Domona. He sat with her throughout the day and all night.

The following winter was particularly harsh. It seemed to Cheveyo that the rain was never going to stop, and it was bitterly cold for California.

Domona never fully recovered from the whipping she had received, and her health began to decline rapidly due to the syphilis she had contracted from the rape, the harsh working conditions they endured, and the poor nutrition.

One day, a trapper arrived at the Mission with a companion who was gravely ill. He rode in and stopped at the chapel. "Senor," he said to a soldier in a broken Russian accent. "Do you have a medical? My friend here is very sick and needs a doctor." The soldier nodded and motioned with his hand to follow him. The trapper drove the horse-drawn cart to the stable. A neophyte took the horse and cart, and two neophytes picked up the sick trapper by the corners of the blanket he was lying on. The trapper started a fit of coughing and moaned in pain.

He was brought into the clinic and placed on a table in the center of the room. The two neophytes who had carried him left the room. One of them ran to Cheveyo in the stable. "Come, you are needed, there is a sick man just brought in and he needs attention. There is no doctor here, only you."

Cheveyo walked into the makeshift clinic. He was shocked at what he saw—a man with big blisters covering his face, arms, and legs. The man was coughing and writhing in pain. He also was drenched in sweat and felt hot to the touch due to a high fever.

Cheveyo looked down at this man and said, "I have not seen this ailment before. I do not know how to treat this man. We can give him water and food if he is hungry. That is all I know to do."

The trapper and Cheveyo lifted the man by his arms and carried the man to a bed against the wall. Cheveyo asked a neophyte in the room to give this man comfort and see that he was given fresh water regularly.

Two days later, the man was dead. Two weeks later, all who had come in contact with the sick man in the room became ill. High fever, vomiting, and a rash that covered the face, arms, and legs and eventually turned into large blisters that broke open and oozed blood.

Dr. Brown was summoned and arrived at the Mission after a few days. He looked at the sick people who filled up the makeshift hospital: soldiers and neophytes alike had come down with the sickness—no one was immune.

"It is smallpox," the doctor announced after he looked at the first patient. "We must quarantine the ill patients immediately."

Cheveyo lay on his mat. The blisters on his face and legs were beginning to turn into scabs when Domona and Luna became sick with it too. The epidemic spread throughout the Mission, taking its toll. Many perished.

Cheveyo tried to make his wife and child as comfortable as possible. It was especially hard to see his little girl so sick; he worried that she could die. Domona had gotten more ill than even he or Luna had. She was already weakened from the lashing she had received and the syphilis that had wracked her body. She did not survive.

The moment his beloved took her last breath, Cheveyo sat with her and cradled her in his arms. Her breathing became harder and more labored as the blisters that lined her throat caused her to suffocate. The night she died, he held her still body all night.

Luna was showing signs of improvement and was soon sitting up and eating small amounts of mashed corn. Both of their faces were etched with deep scars from this terrible disease that wiped out a good portion of the neophyte population of the Mission. Many soldiers lost their lives as well.

It was announced that all bodies were to be put in a cart and driven a league away where a large pit had been dug for burial. Cheveyo wrapped Domona's body in a blanket and gently carried her to the cart that was piled high with dead bodies. He placed her on top and jumped up to the seat to take charge of driving his wife to the designated burial ground.

When he arrived at the burial pit, soldiers were barking orders at the site as there were many carts arriving with bodies and departing to collect more.

Cheveyo was horrified to see that the soldiers were instructing the neophytes to simply toss the men, women, and children's bodies into the pit. Holding the bodies by the feet and hands, the neophytes swung them into the air to land in the pit.

He did not want that for his beloved wife. He took her body down from the cart and placed it on the ground. After all the bodies were removed from the cart, the neophytes walked over to Domona's body.

"No!" shouted Cheveyo. He gently picked her up, still wrapped in the blanket. He walked toward the pit to place her inside. He was walking slowly, carrying her with care. A soldier began shouting at Cheveyo, "Hurry up there! Just toss the body—I have more important things to do with my time!" All the while he was cracking a whip that stung Cheveyo's scarred back. The stinging on his back was nothing in comparison to the pain in his heart at the loss of the love of his life.

Walking still too slowly for the soldier, Cheveyo was almost to the edge of the pit when he tripped over a root sticking up out of the ground. He lost his balance and his hold of Domona. Her body went flying through the air and landed in the pit on top of the pile of dead bodies. The blanket covering her came off, and she lay there with her arms and legs spread, eyes staring blankly into the heavens.

Cheveyo made a move to jump into the pit to retrieve his wife's body and place a blanket around her. The soldier with the whip ran up to him, raising the handle of the whip, and clubbed him over the head. He fell unconscious. Two soldiers picked him up and dragged him to the cart, throwing him into the back of the cart with a thud.

As the cart was headed down the road back to the Mission, Bruno, pushing his horse to top speed, passed the cart. Stopping just short of the death pit, he stared down at the dead body of Domona. He pulled a rose he had picked from the padre's garden out of his waistband, kissed it, and tossed it onto her body as a tear rolled down his cheek.

With half of the population of the neophytes annihilated by the epidemic, it was announced that everyone at the Mission who could walk was to take up the work load, even the children.

From working at the clinic, Cheveyo learned what effect living at the Mission had on the neophytes—the malnourishment, the disease, and the harsh working conditions. How boys as young as ten years were dying from hernias. The overworking of all of the people killed them by the hundreds.

The answer to that, from the Mission's perspective, was to go out into the land and capture more natives and use them to keep the Mission running.

Cheveyo saw abuse of the neophytes regularly. Now that harsh life was to be put upon his daughter. He watched as his wife, a beautiful, vibrant woman, was worked to death, and he swore that this was not going to happen to his child. She was far too young for this.

He made up his mind—it was time to escape. To go back to the life he had led before the Mission. A good life for generations before him. A life that he wanted for his daughter, and he knew his wife would have wanted this too. He wanted Luna to know of his forefather's way of life.

He started to secretly gather food and a small amount of supplies that he would need on his journey back to where he knew not. He was trying not to draw attention to himself and he knew he needed to travel light as he would be traveling with a small child. He knew the right time to escape, the best opportunity to make it happen, was approaching.

There was to be a celebration. People from all the neighboring rancheros were coming to attend the fiesta. It was the celebration of independence from Spain. It took place each year at this time. Flags, flowers, and colorful ribbons were put up all over the Mission. Cattle and chickens were slaughtered and slow-cooked. Frijoles and tamales were being prepared, and many pastries and cakes were being baked. Also, plenty of wine and whiskey was on hand.

The evening had come, and people began to arrive. The party would go on all night. Cheveyo had a plan. He would have Luna wait in their apartment, dressed and ready to go. He had wrapped two blankets, a knife, a leather pouch full water, and some bread with meat in a bundle.

He joined other neophytes in celebration. He made sure that he was seen with a bottle of whiskey, even though he had no intention of drinking any of it. He put the bottle up to his lips to look as though he was drinking it. After a while, he stumbled around, trying to look as drunk as the others were. After stumbling around, he sat down, leaning up against a wall. The neophytes he was drinking with got great joy out of seeing their amigo passed out from the alcohol. Laughing uproariously, they stumbled away from him, leaving him to sleep it off. He wanted for many to see that he was drunk that night so they would not question his not showing up for his stable duties on time the next morning. When the group of drunks left him, he went to his apartment and took Luna by the hand. Making sure they were not seen, they slipped out behind the buildings. It was dark, with just a sliver of moonlight showing the path away from the Mission.

He needed to put as much distance as he could between them and the Mission. Bruno and his soldiers would be after them as soon as they noticed him missing. Bruno was relentless when going after escapees.

He picked up Luna and placed her on his back—she was such a tiny thing for her age—and started running. His leg muscles burning, his lungs gasping, he did not stop until he reached the hilltop above the Mission. He could still faintly hear the music and cheerful voices of the people in the celebrations below. He would go all night and then hide and rest in the daylight.

There was a path into the hills behind the Mission that the cattle used. He decided to stay on this path for tonight. He would have to figure out the best way to stay out of view the next night. His eyes adjusted to the dark, and he could make out figures of cows standing and lying along the path. The uphill climb was exhausting. He had not been this active since he'd lived in his village, and he was a bit older now. Still, he had to keep up the pace to get ahead of Bruno.

He ran uphill as fast as he could with Luna on his back and rested at each plateau. This he did until he finally reached the top.

The downhill descent was much easier. There were more sage bushes on this side of the hill, and they scratched his legs when he rubbed against them. This went on through the night up hills and then down the other side. Taking careful steps, using a long stick as a staff to guide him through the dark, he finally reached the tree-filled valley below. "This will make good cover for us," he said to Luna.

The night started to show its age. He was very tired and needed to rest. The ground had flattened out, and there were many large chaparral shrubs. There were so many that they covered the countryside. He found several chaparral shrubs together that overlapped, forming a large shelter. Cheveyo found one off the path that was about ten feet and looked like a canopy with a small opening that small animals had made tracks into. He looked inside the chaparral dome and was pleased to see that it could provide a hidden shelter for them to rest for this day. He crawled inside and, clearing away some of the dead branches, found it made as good a place as any tule lodge he could make. He spread the blankets on the ground and motioned for Luna to enter as he patted the spot for her to rest with his hand. Luna obeyed and entered. They both fell into a peaceful sleep. Cheveyo was woken by Luna's hand on his chest. He lifted his weary head and heard a rustling outside the chaparral. Cheveyo, getting up on one knee, motioned with his finger over his mouth for Luna to not make a sound. He quietly crept on his hands and knees to the opening of the chaparral dome to take a peak outside. He laughed when he discovered a deer and her doe nibbling on the bush they were hiding in. He motioned for Luna to look at what was making the commotion and when she saw she laughed too. Going back inside, he brought out some food and they ate their first meal as free people.

BRUNO

Bruno opened his eyes, and before he even made a move he knew he had drunk way too much the night before. His head felt like twice its normal size and his mouth was as dry as a desert. He looked to his right and noticed that he was in the stable lying on the straw. He looked to the left and saw a very ugly, fat woman lying next to him. "What took place last night? I don't remember," he said out loud.

He scrambled to his knees, all the while his head pounding like a hammer had been taken to it. He sorted through the pile of clothing, picking out his pants and shirt. Standing up, he leaned against a post to put his pants on. Bruno walked out of the stable, leaving the ugly woman asleep.

The compound was eerily quiet. There were remnants of too much celebration all over the ground. Bruno stumbled to his quarters to sleep away his hangover. Stripping off his pants, he fell face first onto his bed.

By the afternoon, an alcalde knocked loudly on Bruno's door. "Senor Bruno, there has been an escape in the night. That neophyte named Cheveyo who helps Dr. Brown and his daughter are missing," the alcalde said.

Bruno's eyes shot wide open, and he sat up in his bed. Grabbing his pants, he went to the door. "When did you discover this?"

The alcalde shook his head. "He must have left last night during the celebration, sir."

Bruno, infuriated, dismissed the alcalde with a wave of his hand. He finished getting dressed and stormed out to the padre's office.

Bruno burst into the padre's office and blurted out, "Your Grace, there has been an escape. I will set out immediately to recapture the man and his daughter."

The padre, sitting at his desk and writing in his journal, looked up at Bruno. "Ah, Bruno, my son, come in and join me for some tea." The padre motioned with his hand. "I have been meaning to talk to you. It has come to light that the Mexican government no longer wants to support the Missions. You have been a good and faithful servant of the Mission, and I want you to know that you are free to leave to go home to your family, or you may pursue a land grant. The land will be given to the neophytes, but I'm sure that you can gain some of it for yourself."

CHEVEYO

On day two of their trek home, although Cheveyo was uncertain where home was to be, he found a large pine tree with overgrown branches that reached all the way to the ground, making the trunk well hidden from view. "That is where we will stay this day," he said to Luna.

They settled into the center of the tree next to the trunk, breaking off the dead inner branches to create more space. He spread out the blankets and they rested. Evening fell into a beautiful starlit night, and they continued on. The sound of coyotes could be heard howling in the distance. He could see only the eyes of a pack in the dark, and they kept their distance.

Traveling on, they stayed off the cow path and followed alongside a dry creek bed that led them through a canyon. He could make out the shadow of the mountain the soldier had called Cerro Alto de los Bolbones. He had also heard it called the Devil Mountain or Mount Diablo. His people called it Tuyshtak.

He was so happy to see the Tuyshtak in the distance because it meant he was getting close to the place he used to call home. "The Tuyshtak," he told Luna. "It means 'At the Dawn of Time.' This is one of the many things you will learn. I will teach you all about our people."

The dry creek bed ended where it went underground, so they began walking through the valley. The land was flat and sandy with sagebrush in various stages of life.

He saw a skunk scurrying along nearby and threw his knife, killing the skunk before it had a chance to spray its smelly liquid. He carefully cut out the gland that held the liquid and placed it in a piece of cloth cut from his blanket. Luna watched her father with a puzzled look on her face. "This will keep away anything unwanted from us; you will see," he told his daughter.

He felt safe enough now that he decided to rest and continue their journey in the daylight. He found a pit dug into the earth where he supposed a coyote had dug a resting spot, so now it was theirs to use. Cheveyo dug it out a little more to accommodate them. It was just deep enough for himself and Luna to lie flat. He put the blankets down on the ground and instructed Luna to lie down. He gathered some dried tumbleweeds that were awaiting a gust of wind to take them on a journey of their own. He placed the tumbleweeds on top of the pit to cover it, and then before he lay down, he took the gland of the dead skunk. He cut a small slit in the gland and poured out the liquid all around the pit. Gathering more tumbleweeds, he lay down in the pit and gently placed them on top, covering himself and Luna. There they rested until the sun rose its new day gloriously over the land.

"We are almost home!" he excitedly told Luna. They gathered their belongings and began to walk. It was different walking in the daylight but refreshing to Cheveyo. Looking around, he began to recognize some familiar landmarks. They entered the canyon where his brother had been brutally murdered by the soldier for not walking fast enough and being too tired to move on, now so long ago. He did not wish to dwell on bad memories, for this was to be a new beginning. He so wished Domona could be with them.

They reached the old village where he had grown up and where the capture and murder of his people had taken place. It had been a long time since anyone had walked here, yet there was remaining evidence of the violence that had taken place here. Looking around, Cheveyo saw ashes and small bone fragments, the bones of those who should have had a proper burial, but no one was left to do the burying.

Now turning to Luna, he said, "I want you to grow up with the old ways, not the ways of the invaders."

Luna looked up at her father with a smile.

Cheveyo knew they could not stay here long. Bruno would surely be hot on their trail by now. So he motioned to Luna to keep moving. He had heard some recaptured neophytes talking of a place at the foothills where escaped neophytes had gone and lived among the Mountain Tribe. He knew he had to find them and hoped they would take him and his daughter in. If he found this tribe and could live among them, they could live their lives in peace.

BRUNO

Bruno set out the afternoon that they were discovered missing. The hatred he felt for Cheveyo welled up in him, he believed Cheveyo was responsible for the death of his child so he should also die. He did not want Cheveyo getting too far. Riding his horse and leading a second one with supplies, he rode up the path behind the Mission. He said aloud, "I will just take this cow path—that is how they all go. This will be too easy."

He traveled far into the evening without finding any evidence of Cheveyo. He had to stop for the night, as he was getting hungry and was still a little hungover from the previous night's celebrating.

He set up a campfire, cooked some meat, and slept through the night. Waking up to a chilly, cloud-covered morning, Bruno was anxious to get going. He hurriedly gathered his things and set out to find Cheveyo.

The sun broke free of the clouds by late afternoon. Bruno was getting frustrated that he could see no trace of the escapees. He prided himself in his tracking skills. He had to set up a camp again for the night.

The following day, now day three, and still not a trace of Cheveyo and Luna. "Damn it all! How can a neophyte traveling with a small child outsmart me! I am the greatest tracker there is. I do not understand how this can be. When I find him, I'm going to torture him in front of his child for making this so difficult for me!" Bruno said aloud angrily through clenched teeth.

CHEVEYO

Cheveyo led Luna up another slope; he was planning the next night's rest area. The scenery began to look more familiar to him, even though it had been many summers since he had been driven from his home.

The evening sky had the hint of nightfall in the western horizon. They made it up the slope, and looking down he could see a clump of trees just at the bottom of the hill.

"That is where we will rest tonight, my daughter," Cheveyo said. When they got to the bottom of the hill, he entered a tree with branches touching the ground, covering the trunk. He heard the sound of bees buzzing.

"That is what we need," he said, pointing to a hive attached to a limb of the tree high above the ground. He led Luna to the next tree with hanging branches covering the trunk, which was a safe distance from the tree with the swarm of bees hanging from it.

Cheveyo climbed up from the inside of the tree branch by branch until he was far above the ground. He inched his way out onto the limb slowly and carefully so as not to break the branch off. Pulling himself along, he took a stick out of his breeches. Poking at the hive to brake it loose and pushing the stick through, he carefully slid down the branch and jumped down the rest of the way with the hive attached to the stick.

The bees buzzed in a frenzy around the hive. Cheveyo placed the stick with the hive attached in front of the tree they would hide under. No one could search the trunk of this tree without getting attacked by a swarm of bees. He left the hive where it lay and joined Luna to get some rest.

By now, Bruno had figured out that the two had been traveling at night to avoid capture and now felt far enough from the mission to travel in daylight. "He thinks he is smarter than me—ha!" Bruno said aloud. He got off of his horse and stooped down to look at a pair of footprints of a man and a child. "This is their prints! I've got him now. They can't be far."

Getting back on his horse, he rode purposely, guiding his horse to trample the footprints.

He kicked the sides of his horse to ride faster through the canyon and onto the flat plain. Guiding his horse around and through the sagebrush, Bruno could see the figures of a man and a child in the distance. He kicked the sides of his horse to go faster, and with great speed he rode up on Cheveyo and cut off his path. Turning his horse around to face Cheveyo, he said, "You think you can outsmart me? You think you cannot be captured by me?"

Cheveyo placed Luna out of the way and stood up to Bruno in defiance. "I will not be captured. I will not go back!"

Bruno jumped off of his horse and unsheathed a knife in his waistband. He stood in front of Cheveyo with the knife in his hand, ready to stab. "No, you won't be recaptured or taken back, because I'm going to kill you!"

Cheveyo had grabbed his own knife out of its sheath, but now he put his knife down and faced Bruno. "Why are you so hostile toward me? I am not your enemy!"

"You are responsible for the death of my child." Bruno spewed out the words angrily.

"What child? How did I kill your child?"

"The child Domona gave birth to. That was my child. I loved her and I believe she loved me too." Bruno spewed out the words angrily, spit spraying out of his mouth as he spoke.

Cheveyo grasped what Bruno had said with horror. "You! You raped my wife? You gave her the syphilis disease that weakened her body and destroyed her spirit. Your baby was born blind because of the syphilis you gave her. That baby that my wife hated with all of her being because you violated her! She despised the man who did that to her, she despised you! You were not worthy to walk the same ground as my wife!"

Learning this truth filled Cheveyo with rage. It bubbled up and over in him and consumed him. He lunged at Bruno with all of his might, slicing him in the chest. Bruno, stepping back, wiped the blood with his hand. Looking down at his bloodied hand, he looked at Cheveyo with a maniacal grin on his face. He jabbed at Cheveyo with his knife, making contact with the side of Cheveyo's cheek and causing a streak of blood. Cheveyo, ignoring his injury, lunged on top of Bruno, and they both fell to the ground, rolling back and forth, each holding the knifed hand of the other.

Cheveyo knew he was no match for Bruno, but his anger spurred him on. Bruno knew this too, and he jabbed and sliced with the precision of a seasoned warrior.

Cheveyo, now losing blood and weakened from years of malnourishment and overwork, began to falter. He lay on his back with Bruno hovering over him.

Bruno decided to go for the kill. He held the knife in his hand to strike the final blow. He got up on one knee, and as he raised the knife above his head he said, "This is for my chi—"

He was stopped in midsentence by a blow to the back of his head. He put his hand on his head and turned around to see little Luna standing next to him holding a rock in both of her tiny hands. Bruno laughed, and as he turned back to finish off Cheveyo he felt the cold steel of a knife blade pierce his heart. He grabbed the knife and pulled it from his chest. He stared at the bloodied knife in his hand and then at Cheveyo. His eyes rolled up into his head, and he fell to the ground. Cheveyo rolled away as Bruno's body fell over onto his side. A gurgling sound could be heard escaping from Bruno.

Luna dropped the rock to the ground, and it bounced and landed next to Bruno's body.

Cheveyo hugged Luna at Bruno's gravesite. He placed their belongings and Luna on top of one of Bruno's horses. He mounted the other horse and they rode toward the foothills of the Sierras.

They rode for half a day. It was much easier now that they were on horseback. The landscape began to change from dried sand and sage to brush to small, medium, and large pine trees and oaks.

In the distance, Cheveyo saw smoke from a campfire. He dismounted and tied his and Luna's horses up. He crept from the bushes to see where the smoke was coming from. Through his hiding place, he could see it was a campfire, and there was food being cooked but no one was around. It had been abandoned, he surmised.

Getting a closer, look he saw a rabbit on a skewer, and it smelled so good to him. He entered the campsite and stopped at the campfire. Tearing off a piece of the rabbit meat, he turned to walk back to Luna and was met by a man holding a shotgun that was pointed right at him.

"Hold it right there!" the man said.

Cheveyo had seen this kind of man before at the Mission. He was dressed in deerskin pants and had a fur coat, and his language was unfamiliar to Cheveyo. He recognized this man as a trapper, like the one who had brought the sickness to the Mission.

The trapper called out toward the bushes, and a native woman appeared. The trapper said something to her in a native language, and Cheveyo understood the words.

"Ask this Indian where he's from, who he is, and what he's doing out here," the trapper said to the native girl.

"My husband wants to know who you are and what are you doing out here?" the native woman asked.

Cheveyo, so happy to hear a language that he understood answered the native woman. "My daughter and I have escaped from the Mission. We have walked for three nights. We are looking for San Juan. I have heard of a village, a village of the Awaneechee People where he lives—we wish to join him."

The trapper then spoke to Cheveyo in the native language, "We know of this village and visit it often. I will take you to it. First we must eat. Sit we will share our food with you."

The trapper and his wife led Cheveyo and Luna through the Central Valley of California toward the foothills of the Sierra Nevada Mountains. They rode along a path lined with tall pine trees, and soon they found themselves traveling through a thick forest of them.

They reached a clearing by a branch of the Old River that was flowing wildly and was full of trout. The trapper speared several and stuck a stick through the mouths of the trout to bring to the village. Soon they entered the bustling village. There were native men and women in various activities, trappers and traders alike. As they walked through the center of the village, the trapper and his wife were greeted by several natives. He led them to a large lodge of deer skins. A native man exited the lodge.

"Trapper Francois, welcome my brother!" said the native known as Sewati.

"Thank you! I have brought with me some skins and this bunch of fish for fresh horses," the trapper said.

Sewati nodded his head in agreement, taking the stick with the fish hanging from it. "We will talk later."

The trapper pointed to Cheveyo and Luna. "I have brought Cheveyo. He is requesting a meeting with Chief San Juan. He has left the Mission with his daughter and seeks to make a new home here."

Sewati looked at Cheveyo and Luna and said, "Come." He walked them to the lodge and then motioned with his hand, saying, "Wait here."

Sewati entered the lodge and in a few minutes returned. "San Juan will see you."

Cheveyo entered the lodge as Luna stayed with the trapper and his wife.

Cheveyo was greeted by a group of native men in a circle. At the head of the circle was San Juan. He looked up at Cheveyo and instantly recognized him from the Mission.

"Cheveyo, my brother, sit. I last saw you at the Mission, when I asked you to leave with me. I am glad that you have decided to," said San Juan.

Cheveyo, pleased that he was remembered by San Juan, spoke to him and the council members. "I have left the Mission in the dark of night with my daughter after the death of my wife. There was an illness that killed many. The padre ordered all to work, including the young children. I have seen what the hard work has done to the children too young to be worked so hard and without nourishment to sustain any life. I decided that I wanted my child to know the way of life of my father and the fathers before him. I come seeking you to ask you and your council to allow us to join you here and make this our home."

Chief San Juan looked at Cheveyo. "The council and I will vote. Paytaw, take Cheveyo and his daughter to my lodge. My wife will give you food. We will let you know of our decision."

He followed Paytaw out of the lodge to a smaller lodge with a large native woman bent over a cook fire. Cheveyo and Luna sat down at the fire to await the decision.

San Juan exited the lodge with the council members in tow. The village people gathered around the chief and council members, and San Juan summoned Cheveyo and Luna. When the pair appeared in front of the chief and was surrounded by the people of the village, Chief San Juan spoke to the people.

"My people, Cheveyo and his daughter Luna have escaped from the Mission as most of us here have done. They have come to us wanting to join our village. The council and I have decided to let this happen. All of us here have been in his place. The white man calls us "all one." We are called this because we have joined in and blended with the ones of many tribes that have survived the Mission. We will let the people decide. Do we let them join us?"

With a unanimous agreement the village people answered, "Yes!"

"So be it!" shouted San Juan, as all the people cheered and howled in merriment.

Cheveyo and Luna were given a lodge that they shared with another small family. Luna blossomed with the freedom of village life. Cheveyo taught her their language. He taught her that they were a tribelet of the Northern Valley Yokuts, a peaceful people who had lived in this valley for thousands of years. He taught her to gather berries and tule roots to use for shelter and making of baskets and mats for sleeping. He taught her to sew rabbit furs to use as clothing as the weather grew cold. Luna thrived in her new environment.

The land in the valley was not the same was it was before the Mission. The cattle had eaten up or trampled all the vegetation that the natives used to use as food. So the tribes had no choice but to go on raids of the new settlements and capture cows for food and horses to ride.

Cheveyo went on many of these raids with the others in his village. The raids were against the rancheros that sprouted up from the land that was divided up and given to families and friends of the current government.

This peaceful existence did not last long. More settlers were moving into the area. They killed off the remaining small animals, including rabbits and squirrels, that the tribe used for clothing and food. They left remnants of the cast-aside belongings that they no longer wanted. Soon the land was littered with the white man's refuse and trash; this problem continued to grow.

The people were very generous with sharing food with the new settlers. They traded furs and seeds for tools and horses, but they also brought also whiskey and disease.

Malaria and yellow fever spread throughout the village and wiped out a large number of its members. The Mexican soldiers that replaced the Spanish soldiers battled the village, trying to keep the tribes from raiding the rancheros and new settlements. The tribe's water supply became poisoned and useless due to the grazing cattle on the land.

Cheveyo and his new tribesmen had to go on raids just to keep from starving. The people in the village did what they had to do to survive.

Changes continued for the natives. The people who entered the village came from all walks of life: Awaneechee, Miwok, Yokutes, Californios, and natives who were raised up in the Mission, lost in a world no longer their own to intermarriages of Spanish and Mexican. There were also natives who went to work on the rancheros after leaving the Mission only to receive little to no pay and further abuse from the settlers that poured into the land. Also, a new breed of white men—dishonest and bloodthirsty—hiding in the lawlessness of the Wild West.

Drought years followed by heavy rains and flooding made the struggle just to survive harder still for the natives. A new measles epidemic swept through the village, killing many. Most of the native women's bodies were ravaged by syphilis, which left them unable to produce offspring.

Battles against the Americans and Mexico raged on in small skirmishes throughout Alta California for the control of California. A captain in the American army came to recruit men of the village to help in the fight against Mexico.

Cheveyo, Sula, Medu, and Juaquin all joined the Americans and were to receive payment of twenty-five dollars per month. The payment never came, however, so they abandoned the Americans' fight in disgust.

The American soldiers were not paid either, so thefts of horses from the village became more common. This led to an escalation of raids on the settler's ranches for horses and cattle, led by Cheveyo.

The new settlers that poured into the area demanded that the United States military do something to stop the raids that were going on against their ranches that were sprouting up along the territory of Alta California.

The United States government then appointed agents to be liaisons between the American settlers and the people of the village who were slowly losing the very land they called home. The agents went to the village to negotiate with the tribe to get them to stop raiding the ranches of the new settlers.

The Mexican war ended with the signing of a treaty and a sum of money paid that was well under value. This was the beginning of the United States' rule of Alta California. However, this did not change the status of the native peoples in the eyes of the Americans—to them, natives were savages, unable to learn or govern themselves. So the order was given by the United States government to shoot and kill any natives raiding settlers' ranches. The natives had no other food source, so they had to continue to raid the ranches and the new settlers' homesteads. The United States government's answer was to corral the natives and move them onto reservations.

Luna grew into a beautiful and strong woman. She had many suitors. However, only one young buck caught her eye. His name was Otaktay. He was from a tribe of the Central Valley Yokuts that lived in the village. He pursued Luna and presented Cheveyo with wild horses, which he had captured to show his strength; deer and rabbit meat, which he had hunted in the highest part of the mountains to show Cheveyo that he would be a good provider; and shells of the finest quality, which he had traded for to make a necklace to show that he treasured Luna. Cheveyo agreed that he would be a good provider for his daughter, and they were joined together in marriage.

Cheveyo could see that Otaktay loved his daughter very much, and he was pleased. He thought about how Domona would have loved seeing her daughter so happy.

After a while, Cheveyo learned that he was to be a grandfather.

The months passed, and Luna grew large with child. The impending birth was much anticipated.

After a long cold winter, the meat had run out, and the people were hungry. The tribe needed to go on a raid. The only food available to the village was the cattle from the ranches that had taken over the land. Only the men young enough and who could ride a horse and shoot an arrow were to go on the raid. Though Cheveyo was getting older, he could still ride a horse and hunt with the best of them. It was getting harder for him to move fast, however, and it took great speed to steal cattle and get away quickly.

On this raid, Cheveyo and Otaktay rode behind Paytaw and Sewati. San Juan led the group to a ranchero that was over the mountain to the west. They rode up a steep incline, reminding Cheveyo that this was the way the soldiers had come that day that they had destroyed his village so long ago. With great speed, down into the valley the raiding party rode, coming up on some cattle grazing in a field within sight of the ranchero. Moving fast, they each took to the opposing side of a fat cow, trapping it between their horses. Otaktay aimed his bow and arrow true and shot straight into the heart of the beast. It fell to the ground, twitching. Cheveyo and Sewati were so pleased that they stopped and raised their bow and arrows, giving a whooping cry of joy at the thought that they would be eating this night.

Just then Cheveyo heard an unfamiliar sound—something like the buzz of a bee—and then saw a small puff of smoke on Otaktay's chest. He grabbed his chest and fell off of his horse to the ground. Cheveyo jumped off of his horse and, as the rest of his group turned to run away, he grabbed Otaktay and threw him up onto his horse sideways, jumped into the saddle, and sped away with that sound of buzzing whipping past his ears.

They rode their horses as fast as they could, without taking any of the spoils of the hunt.

They didn't stop until they were on the other side of the steep incline, a safe distance from the ranchero. They looked at Otaktay. He was dead, with a bullet through his heart.

Cheveyo was saddened to have to tell his daughter that her husband had died, but he reminded her that providing for the village was an honorable way to die and that he would be remembered as a warrior.

When he got back to the village, he could not find Luna.

"What has become of my daughter?" he asked the woman cooking tule roots outside the lodge. The toothless woman looked up at Cheveyo and, smiling, pointed to the forest. "She went to have her baby."

LUNA

Luna's baby boy was born on the night the coyotes were howling at the big red moon high in the sky. Luna sat among the dried grass and looked down at her baby boy as he suckled at her breast. She felt so much joy and could not wait for her husband to get back from the raid to name him.

She lay there until morning, too tired from the birthing to get up. When she walked back to her lodge, she saw a gathering of people around Cheveyo.

"Where is Otaktay?" Luna asked. "He needs to meet his baby boy."

Cheveyo was overjoyed at the birth of his grandson, but at the same time he was saddened that now he had to tell Luna of the demise of her husband. He took Luna aside from the crowd.

"Papa, is something wrong? Tell me, Papa, is it my husband?" Luna asked her father.

"There was a shooting. Otaktay is dead," he said to his daughter with tears welling up in his eyes.

Luna, weak from the birthing and hearing this unbelievable news, dropped to her knees. She began wailing and rocking her baby. "How could this be? What happened to my husband? Where is he? I want to see him!" Cheveyo helped Luna up and helped her to her lodge.

"He is here. I will take the baby." He reached for the boy, and Luna held him all the more closely.

"No!" cried Luna. "No. I want him to meet his boy!"

Luna stared down at the baby boy for a minute but then handed him to her father. She went into the lodge, and the dim light from the fire pit revealed her dead husband's body lying on a tule mat. She knelt down next to him. She loved him so much. It was so hard to see him lying dead. She took a shell that was placed by the body and, grabbing handfuls of her waist-length hair, began to cut it off. Strand by strand, she kept cutting until there was none left.

The next day, the village gathered around Chief San Juan to name the baby of Otaktay and Luna. The chief held the baby up in the air and said, "The night you were born, the coyotes sang in praise of your birth. You shall be called Caniday. It means you are one with the coyote—a great honor." He handed the cooing baby back to Luna. She wrapped the boy snugly in a rabbit blanket.

Then Cheveyo, Luna, and the whole village, led by Chief San Juan, walked out to a clearing where they buried Otaktay.

The little family, Cheveyo, Luna, and Caniday lived peacefully among the Awaneechee. This village was made up of people from all different tribes and mixed native-Spanish-Mexican. All were welcomed to this friendly Tribe. They survived by trading for furs and tools.

Caniday toddled around and was taught the old ways by Cheveyo. "I will teach him to hunt and fish and the ways of my fathers before me. I will tell him the stories I learned as a child."

Luna just smiled at her father.

Hunting began to be more of a challenge as settlers trickled in from America. Their cattle continued to eat all the vegetation and soil the drinking water.

Trappers came and went into the village, a stopover for rest and trading their goods. One Trapper brought news to Chief San Juan and the council members of more settlers coming and grabbing land to farm, for the very land they were living on.

One day, some Mission Indians that Cheveyo knew wandered into the village—several men, women, and children. They had gone north to Fort Sutter, which was owned by a Dutchman. They told Chief San Juan that the Dutchman was cruel and worked the neophytes that had left the Mission very hard and withheld pay.

Raids on settlements continued. The tribesmen stole horses and cattle that grazed on the land that the people of the village used to hunt. On one of the raids, three of the tribesmen were captured and imprisoned in the same Mission that Cheveyo had escaped from.

Chief San Juan called a meeting of the men of the village. "Three of our brothers have been taken to the Mission as prisoners. Are we to go get them?" the chief asked the council members.

"I say we go get them!" Cheveyo voted. As did Sula, Manwell, and Mobe, all escaped neophytes of the Mission.

They rode on horseback early the next morning to gain the element of surprise. The sun was barely peeking over the mountains on the horizon. The men gained speed as they rode and got closer to the Mission.

They burst through the entrance of the now-dilapidated buildings of the Mission. Time had not been kind to it. The Mission was in great disrepair and had been pillaged. Cheveyo had mixed feelings about being there. So many bad memories were here for him, but also the body of his wife was buried here. His only comfort was in knowing that her beautiful spirit was free.

They rode to a building that was still intact, with a ranchero guard in front of the door. The group pushed through the door, pushing past the guard. There was a guard inside who was easily overtaken, and the door to the room that held the three tribesmen was broken down. Their rescuers waiting on horseback, the three imprisoned tribesmen jumped on backs of horses, and with great speed they all escaped back to the village.

Gold was discovered at Sutter's Fort. The cry of "Gold!" was heard throughout the land, and soon hundreds of thousands of men flooded into the territory of California, still not part of the United States, to seek their fortune.

They came over land, through every mountain and canyon, and by sea, abandoning the ships when they landed in the harbor of San Francisco Bay and leaving a graveyard of empty ships bobbing in the water. The flood of incoming wagons and men on horseback was unstoppable.

Cheveyo decided it would be a good idea to go to the mines and try to gather some gold to feed his family. He and Sula, Manwell, Juaquin, and August packed some tools and went to Coloma, a mining town that had spouted up.

Arriving at the camp in Coloma was a whole new world for the group. There was a cluster of wooden cabins and canvas lodges with food supplies and tools. There was an abundance of saloons and Monte banks in this mining town. Continuing through the town, they arrived at the bank of the south fork of the American River. All around them men were panning for gold. It seemed like hundreds of them. Cheveyo had never seen so many white men at one time, and he felt a little apprehensive…rightfully so.

The group settled on a spot that was not occupied. The day was very hot, and Cheveyo was parched, but the water was not fit to drink. He was also very hungry. They were here only to gather the yellow rock that was so much in demand now—the rock that turned men into animals, it seemed to Cheveyo.

Manwell and Sula began to hoot with excitement. They had easily found some of the gold nuggets just at their fingertips. Cheveyo dipped his pan into the river and retrieved a dusting himself. "This is so easy!" Cheveyo gleefully shouted to August.

"Hey, you diggers! This is our claim—you is trespassin'! Now git! Go on, git, afore I put a hole in your gut!" yelled a miner. Cheveyo looked at the white man with a red and white checkered shirt and suspender holding grey wool pants, brown boots, and a straw hat who came running up to the group waving a shotgun. "You savages ain't got no business in these parts!" the miner yelled at Cheveyo.

He did not understand the man's language, but he understood the tone all too well. He looked at his companions and motioned with his head to head out. They picked up their meager belongings and walked farther upstream, away from any people, where they figured it was safe. More gold was pulled out of the river by all.

That evening, they went into the town of Coloma to cash in their gold and buy some food. The assay office was crowded, and the agent was paying out in cash to the miners for their find of the day. The miners then quickly went to the saloons and played Monte all night.

Cheveyo stepped up to the assay agent, who placed the gold weighing scale under the counter and brought up a different one that paid a lesser amount for the gold than what the white man had received.

Taking their cash in hand, they next went to the general store, a canvas-tented building next to the assay office. They gathered various supplies that they would need and paid the storekeeper, oblivious to the fact that they paid more than a white man purchasing the same items. They took their purchases and went back out to the river where they had been earlier that day, only to find two white squatters at the site.

Cheveyo put his supplies down and sat down on a log next to the river where the two white men sat. The white man looked at Cheveyo. "This here's our claim," he said as he pulled a long knife out of his belt and waved it in the air.

Cheveyo, a peaceful and patient man, picked up his things and moved a little farther down the river. Yet another white man shouted to Cheveyo and his group, "That is our claim too, move out!" The miner charged toward Cheveyo with a knife.

Cheveyo, not wanting to fight, picked up his things, and the group walked upstream and settled down for the night.

The next morning, Cheveyo woke to a mob of white men approaching and shouting, holding up guns and knives. The leader, who was followed by the two miners who had chased them away from the first camp, came charging up to Cheveyo and pointed at Sula and Manwell.

"These two savage diggers have stolen Clem's tools," he said, pointing to one of the miners. "We don't take kindly to thieves around here!" the man accused.

Cheveyo didn't know what to think. He stood up quickly, as did Manwell, Sula, August, and Juaquin. The mob charged toward the group, but Cheveyo was too fast and ran with the others trailing behind. Gunshots were heard and bullets buzzed by Cheveyo's ears. Manwell and Sula, who were running behind Cheveyo, fell to the ground, and the mob converged upon them. Cheveyo and Juaquin ran faster, and August passed them both. They kept running until they were safely out of range. They reached town and wandered around until they saw a stable where they took refuge. They noticed a native working in the stable.

Cheveyo approached him and asked in native language, "Do you speak Cholvon?"

The native just stared at Cheveyo.

"Habla Español?" Cheveyo asked.

The stable hand spoke. "Si, Señor."

Cheveyo explained what had just taken place at the mines. The stable native listened intently and then nodded his head.

"I want to seek justice for my brothers; I fear they have been killed by a mob of white miners," Cheveyo said.

"There is no justice for us," the stable native said. "A native cannot press any charges against a white man. It is the white man's law, and here you are in a white man's world. If you want the gold, you have to work for the white man—it is the only way. Go to that lodge there." He pointed to a wooden shack. "There you will find a man who will pay you to dig his gold. That is the only way you can gain anything around here."

Cheveyo felt frustrated and bewildered. He did not want to return to the village without gaining something to show for his efforts. He thanked the stable hand.

"Should we go see the white man to work for him?" Cheveyo asked August and Juaquin.

"Yes," replied August. "If for nothing else for our dead brothers."

The three walked across the dirt road and entered the wooden shack.

Sitting in a chair behind a desk, a fat white man with a long white beard, rosy red cheeks, and curly wisps of grey hair spilling out of his hat wrote in a journal with a quill pen. Sweeping the floor in the corner, a native boy was busy at work. The white man looked up from his desk and then back down at his journal.

"You Injuns speak English?" the fat man asked.

The trio stood motionless in front of the fat man's desk. Without looking up, the fat man shouted, "Boy! Come over here and translate. The boy speaks Injun and English."

The native boy began translating what the man said in the Miwok language. "I am Mr. James. I hire Injuns to work the mines for me. You do the digging for me and give me what you find, and you will be paid. If you're interested, make your mark on this paper."

Cheveyo nodded at August and Juaquin. He stepped up and put an X on the sheet of paper that was presented in front of him. August and Juaquin did the same.

Mr. James took the signed papers and put them in a drawer in the desk. "Boy, give these three some tools, a pan, and a map. Show them where to go to start digging." Mr. James waved his hand in the air. The native boy ran across the room and came back with the shovels and pans and handed them to the trio. He motioned with his hand and they followed him to the river just outside of town.

"Here." The native boy pointed to a trail. He gave them the map and instructed them where to go. They followed the trail until they saw a group of other native men panning in a river.

The work was long, hot, and grueling. They panned for gold all day and into the night. Tired and sore at the end of the day, they just wanted to get some food. They went back to the wooden shack. Mr. James was still sitting at the desk. "Well, let's see how you did today."

The native boy told them to place the gold that they had panned that day on the scale on Mr. James's desk. Mr. James sat back and smiled. "You Injuns did good today! You earned your pay. Boy, get them their pay."

The native boy ran off and returned with three pairs of denim overalls, worn dirty and patched in spots. He handed one pair to Cheveyo, one to August, and one to Juaquin.

Cheveyo looked at the overalls, puzzled, and looked at the native boy. "What is this? Where is the gold payment? We want to be paid in gold!"

The native boy looked at Cheveyo and then at Mr. James. "They want gold payment," the boy said.

Mr. James laughed a hearty laugh, his fat belly jiggling. "This is the payment. It says so right on the paper that you signed, right here. Mr. James pulled out the paper from the desk drawer. He pointed to a place on the paper where it said what the payment was for a day's work. "See here, that is where it says what you will be paid. One pair of overalls. Now get out before I throw you out. I'm a busy man."

Cheveyo, a peaceful man, became enraged. He lunged across the desk at Mr. James. Mr. James, for being a fat man, was quick and dodged. Cheveyo fell over the desk and rolled on the floor, ending in a standing position. Mr. James pulled a gun out from his waistband and put it in Cheveyo's face, pressing it on his nose. "This was a fair deal. You signed a contract, and I honored it," Mr. James said through clenched teeth. "Now get out of my office before I fill you full of lead."

Cheveyo stood up, picking the overalls up with him. He threw them at Mr. James and walked out.

Cheveyo walked across the dirt street to a saloon. He stood outside and peered in the window. There were several tables full of drunk and obnoxious men playing Monte. Many more drunk men stood at the bar. At one of the tables where the men were playing cards, Cheveyo watched a fight break out. The gamblers' loud voices could be heard above all the voices in the saloon. He heard screams and a chair falling over as people scattered away from the arguing gamblers. The music stopped playing. One of the arguing gamblers stood up, and with a fast motion of his hands, shot his gun at the gambler sitting across the table from him, who fell backward out of his chair and lay motionless on the floor. The saloon keeper walked to the dead gambler, grabbed his feet, and dragged him out to the back of the saloon. The music and loud voices resumed as if nothing had just happened.

Cheveyo decided right then that the gold rush was not for him. He wanted to go back home to his village.

Cheveyo, August, and Juaquin did not waste any time. They headed out of town that night on foot. The journey would take several days. He thought of Luna and Caniday. It had been days since he had last seen them.

Heading southeast through the Central Valley of California, they passed small settlements that dotted the countryside. Cheveyo, August, and Juaquin took care to avoid them. They were not looking for trouble.

After two days, they reached the foothills of the Sierras, where August knew of a tribe of Ohlones—a village where they could feel safe and get some food and much-needed rest.

On approaching the Ohlones's village they heard an all too familiar sound. The sound of gunfire and panic-driven screaming.

They crept slowly to the edge of the village, staying under cover. They were horrified at what they saw. A squad of white degenerates called Rough Riders, rejects from the armed forces of the United States, had found a perfect environment for their marauding ways, rampaging through the village of the Ohlones. The dead bodies lay in various positions throughout the village.

Cheveyo witnessed a small child toddling toward its mother, crying in fright, being taken over and cut down with an axe by one of the Rough Riders. Then the mother's head was cut in two by the same axe. He witnessed a baby being thrown into the raging river nearby, bobbing up and down in the rapids.

When the Rough Riders were satisfied that they had killed the entire village, they walked around the pillaging and cutting off scalps of the dead bodies for trophies.

He heard one them say "I've got ten of these scalps. At two bucks a head I'm making a killing! Ha! Get it? Making a killing! Ha-ha!"

The other Rough Rider looked at him and shook his head. "Just gather the scalps and let's get out of here."

The scalps were taken off of every man, woman, and child of the village. The Rough Riders tied them onto their saddles and rode off.

Cheveyo looked at August and Juaquin, still hiding in the bushes. "We must get back to our village now!"

They started to run and did not stop until they arrived at the edge of their village. They went straight to the chief's lodge. A council meeting was taking place. Cheveyo spoke urgently. "Chief San Juan, I have just come from a village in the valley where I saw men, women, and children slaughtered before my own eyes. The white man is killing the women and children!"

Chief San Juan listened intently to Cheveyo's descriptions of the events that he, August, and Juaquin had witnessed earlier that day.

Chief San Juan listened to every word, shook his head in disbelief, and then spoke to the men in the lodge. "We had gotten word by the French trappers that came through last full moon. They spoke of a battalion called Mariposa. These are bad men getting paid by the white man to bring in scalps of our people. So it has come to light." Chief San Juan stared into the fire pit as he spoke. "We must protect our women and children. We will move higher into the mountains called Sierra. We will go so far they cannot touch us. We will gather extra meat and hides to prepare for a new village. This is what we must do. When winter is over, we will leave here."

Everyone sitting at the council fire agreed that they would prepare themselves for a move to the Sierras after the winter. Autumn was upon them, and the weather was still mild and warm, good raiding weather.

There was talk of going on a raid for horses and cattle in the coming days to have a good start on storing extra meat and hides.

"Chief San Juan," Cheveyo spoke privately, "I am an old man now. I will only hold up the young warriors. I will not go on this raid but will stay here and help make other preparations."

"Cheveyo, my son, you have proven yourself to be a great warrior many times. It is good that you are wise enough to know this and not risk your life. We need strong men like you to stay and protect the village too." The chief put his hand on Cheveyo's shoulder. "Now go see your daughter and tell her that we are going soon."

Over the next few months, Luna and Caniday did their part in gathering nuts of the oak trees and wild berries that grew in large bushes in the fields. Cheveyo watched as his grandson

Caniday was growing and taught him the ways of his people. He taught him their language, which had been spoken by the tribe for thousands of years. Caniday was a fast learner. He had even learned to speak some English from a trapper at the village while Cheveyo was out in the mining fields. He showed him how to set traps for rabbits and squirrels, how to hunt and catch fish in the stream, and how to make a shelter. "These are the things a warrior needs to know. They were taught to me by my father before he was killed. So when you become a man one day, you will be prepared. It is good how you look after your mother. Someday you will have to provide for her, as I am getting too old to hunt. Now I grow tired and need rest." Cheveyo waved his hand for Caniday to leave.

The months that followed were busy for the village people. There was much gathering of whatever they could in the way of food for the winter and gathering for the move to higher safer ground.

After the raids, the cowhides of the cattle had to be scraped, dried, and stretched. The extra horses were slaughtered and the meat dried. There was a great need for many hides. The winters were much colder in the Sierras, with deep snowfall, unlike the valley, where they had only rain.

Cheveyo helped in the gathering of tules that would be needed to make new lodges, while Luna and Caniday spent their days gathering berries and nuts.

One warm autumn day, as the leaves were turning orange and red, Luna and Caniday were getting ready to gather more berries. "Go tell your grandfather that we are going over the next hill today. There is a fresh patch that is bursting with berries! Get an extra basket too. I want to fill all the baskets so we will be done with it."

"Okay, Mama," chimed Caniday in English. Luna looked at him with raised eyebrows.

Luna watched with pride as her son ran off. "I suppose it is good for him to know English," Luna said aloud.

Sitting outside his tule lodge basking the warmth of the sun, enjoying the beauty of his life in this village, Cheveyo watched the children run by as they played and the women cooked and chatted among themselves. He was content with his life. His daughter Luna having grown up knowing the old ways and his grandson now eight summers.

Most of the men from the village were out on a raid. He and a few of the grandfathers stayed behind. Perking up his ears, he thought he heard a scream that sounded like Luna's. Then, to his horror, he saw Caniday running into the village, rushing past the chatting women straight toward him.

"Grandpa! Grandpa! Come quick! The white men are taking Mama!" Caniday breathlessly yelled to Cheveyo.

Cheveyo jumped up and met Caniday part way. "Show me where she is!" he commanded as he ran with the boy. Caniday directed him up the ridge.

Upon reaching the top of the ridge, Cheveyo stopped short to see two white men on horseback riding back and forth, corralling the screaming Luna. She dodged the men as they tried to grab her by the arms.

"No!" Cheveyo yelled as he broke into a full run at the men on horseback. This allowed a distraction for Luna, and she bolted into the brush. One of the men saw Luna running for the bushes and kicked the sides of his horse, catching up to her. Running his horse alongside her, he scooped her up by the hair and the scruff of her tunic. Luna screamed as she was pulled up and draped over the horse sideways. The horseman kicked the sides of the horse, sending it into a full gallop.

Cheveyo ran after the man who had his daughter, reaching out with his arms in a desperate attempt to stop that horseman from getting away. The hope of catching her faded with every step as the horseman rode away.

The other horseman behind Cheveyo pulled his rifle out of its sheath on his saddle. As Caniday ran toward his grandfather, the horseman took aim and shot his rifle, missing Cheveyo. Caniday reached his grandfather, and Cheveyo grabbed him in a tight hold to his breast and began to run for the cover of the bushes. Cheveyo felt a punch to his right shoulder and was propelled forward, falling to the ground while still holding Caniday in his arms. Adrenaline surged through his body, and he jumped up with Caniday and started to run. They were almost at the bushes that would shield them from harm when Cheveyo felt a white hot blow to his back that he could feel through his entire chest. He fell to the ground again, this time on top of Caniday.

Cheveyo, lying on top of Caniday, began to sputter and gasp. A surge of blood gushed from his mouth, and it became harder to take in life-sustaining air.

Coughing and sputtering and struggling to speak, Cheveyo whispered to Caniday with his last labored breath. "Do not move, no matter what, lie still." Then, his last shallow breath taken, Cheveyo was gone.

Always minding what his grandfather told him to do, Caniday lay as still as death.

The white man on horseback rode over to the two bodies. He put his rifle back in its holder and slithered off his horse. Leaning over Cheveyo, he called out to his partner, who had Luna, "Look at this, Clem, I got two with one shot!"

Taking out his knife, he stood over the body of Cheveyo. Grabbing a handful of Cheveyo's hair he pulled up his body, arching his back, and began to slice his scalp like a turkey on Thanksgiving. He cut Cheveyo's scalp from the forehead to the nape of the neck. Cheveyo's lifeless body fell with a thump down onto Caniday. The man tucked the bloody scalp into his belt and was reaching for Caniday's hair when the other horseman, who had Luna on his horse, returned.

"Come on, Jenkins! We got what we came for. Leave those Injuns and let's git before the whole tribe comes after us." Clem, the man who had captured Luna, who was kicking and screaming, turned his horse and rode away.

Caniday lay still under the lifeless body of his grandfather, listening for the two men to ride away. He wriggled out from under his grandfather's body, tears mixing with dirt and forming streaks on his young face, and called out, "I will find you, Mama!"

The day after the tribe held a ceremony for the burial of Cheveyo. The Mariposa Battalion marched into the village led by Colonel Jackson.

The Battalion peacefully gathered the village people. San Juan, now too old to fight, walked with his people to the reservation.

Caniday stood looking at his grandfather's body, realizing he was dead, began walking in the direction the two white men had gone. He decided he would go find his mama. He had to find her.

Following the path the horses had made, he began to walk.

Walking for hours in the hot sun, he noticed his feet making puffs of dust fly into the air. He started to stamp his feet as he walked to see how high he could make the little puffs fly up. He was so thirsty, and this took his mind off of his thirst for a while.

Still looking down at the puffs of dust he was creating, he did not notice a white man in a horse-drawn wagon approaching.

The man in the wagon pulled up next to Caniday. "Well now, young'un, what you be about heh?" he asked.

"I am looking for my mama; two men stole her, and I am going to find her," he stated.

The white man looked the boy up and down. Holding the reins of his horse, he licked his lips. "Well, you must be thirsty; come on up here and I will give you some water and take you to your mama. I am Jeb. What's your name, sonny?'

"I am Caniday. It is the name of the coyote. Mama said it means a strong man. You really know where my mama is?" asked Caniday as he climbed up on the wagon and sat next to Jeb.

the horse to proceed. "Sure 'nuff." "Why sure 'nuff, young'un, we will go see her right now," Jeb said as he commanded

They rode on down the dusty road until the sun was high in the afternoon sky. The destination was unknown to Caniday. Sitting up so high on the wooden bench of the cart, he could take in the scenery of the countryside, even through the dust kicked up by the rolling wheels of the cart.

Jeb looked down at Caniday and smiled a toothless grin. He was the son of a preacher man back in his hometown in the East. His father had taught the good book, and Jeb had run from it. He was as mean and black-hearted as they come. He only did what served his purpose, and his purpose was no good.

In the distance, Caniday could see a lodge that was made out of wood. There was a man standing outside the doorway of the wooden shack smoking a cigarette.

"Hey, Jeb, whatcha got there?" the smoking man asked as he spit into the dirt.

"Hey, Jim, I got me a little varmint that will get me enough money to set up a shop at the mines." Jeb grinned. Can we go inside? It's hot as blazes out here."

Loud shouts and laughter could be heard from inside the wooden shack, and as the cart got closer the sound got louder. Caniday looked up at Jeb with a puzzled look. "You just follow me now, don't stray," Jeb said.

Jeb pulled up on the reins and the horse stopped. He jumped down from the cart and tied the reins to a post. "Well, come on then." He motioned with his hand, and Caniday jumped down and followed Jeb inside the wooden lodge.

As they entered the shack, all Caniday could see was a wall of men standing with their backs to the door and rows of wooden benches with an aisle down the center. The sound of the men in the room was almost deafening. Jeb pushed his way through the middle aisle that was filled with the sea of men. He made his way to the front of the room with Caniday at his heels. There, he stepped onto a two-foot platform, spun around, and with one quick motion hoisted Caniday up on the stage. Caniday stood looking down at the sea of white bearded faces, all shouting and laughing. He did not stand alone for long. A door on the side of the stage opened, and a parade of women one by one was ushered into the room. They were naked and dirty. The first three to walk out had the whitest skin he had ever seen and their eyes were just slits. "How do you see out of those eyes?" Caniday asked one. She ignored him and walked to the edge of the stage. Next, a brown-skinned girl walked up, and then a native girl he recognized as one of the young girls from his village.

"Keely!" Caniday shouted at her above the roar of the men in the audience. "Have you seen my mama?" She stared at him blankly.

"Okay, settle down now, settle down! Let's start the bidding! What do I get for these China girls? Over here. Fresh young girls from China. There is a high demand for the Chiny these days. What am I bid?"

The three naked girls stood next to each other, trying to cover their bodies with their arms.

"I'll start!" yelled a man in the audience. "I'll give twenty dollars for all three of 'em."

"Twenty-five!" yelled another.

"Thirty dollars in gold!" shouted another.

The room went silent. "Do I hear thirty-five?" No one spoke. "Thirty, going once, going twice, sold for thirty to the man with the brown hat! Pay the man at the side of the stage." The next girl to be displayed was a young girl stolen from her family home in Mexico.

"Next, we have this fine young Mexican girl, she ain't much to look at, but then who's looking at the face? Eh? What am I bid?"

The sound of laughter filled the room. The bidding went on until a price and buyer were had. Next, Keely was up for bid.

Again Caniday asked Keely, "Have you seen my mama?"

Before she could answer, Jim stepped up to Caniday. "I'll show you your mama," he said, and with his booted foot he gave Caniday a kick in the behind that sent him tumbling across the floor of the stage. Howls of laughter filled the room, and someone shouted out, "Hey, Jim, don't damage the merchandise!" More laughter filled the room.

"What am I getting for this squaw? She is young and healthy and full of spunk. Why it took two men to catch this one. What is the opening bid?"

"I bid ten dollars," a man in the audience shouted. Nobody else bid on Keely.

Keely was led out of the room by her purchaser and turned to give a last look at Caniday. He then stood alone on the stage. "What am I bid for this young'un?" Jim asked the crowd.

"He looks kind of puny to me," a man in the crowd called out.

"Ya he don't look like he could lift a chicken!" yelled another.

"I'll give you two dollars for the little skunk," said a tall man in the back of the room.

"Now come on, fellas, this here is a prime young buck. Sure, he's small now, but you can train him in the way you want and he'll be a good workhorse for years to come. He will give you many years of good hard work," cried Jim.

"I'll give you two cents for that one," a man called out. The room broke out in a wave of laughter.

Another man called out, "If he's so valuable, you take him, Jim!" More laughter in the room.

Frustrated, Jim held up Caniday's head by the chin. "All right, sold for two dollars!"

Another voice yelled out, "That's a dollar ninety too much!" Again a burst of laughter from the room.

"All right, it's been a long day and I need to get home. Pay the man at the side of the stage."

The man who had bought Caniday was Caleb. He was a farmer who had moved out from the East Coast and tried to make it rich panning for gold. When that didn't work out, he had bought land that was being sold by the government. The land belonged to a family that gained it after the Mission closed down. He had forced the family off the land by ambushing the man of the house. When his widow couldn't provide papers of ownership, he drove the widow and her six children back south were they were from. "Just business," he would say to the men he gambled with in the town of Stockton, the nearest town that had grown from a port entryway to the mines into a bustling and growing town.

Caleb looked at Caniday. "Well, come on then, I expect a full day's work out of you."

"Where are we going, mister? I need to look for my mama," Caniday stammered.

"Oh, hell no, I just paid two dollars for you, you belong to me now, and you can call me sir." Caleb grabbed his arm and half dragged him, half pulled him along to his horse, which was tied up to a hitch outside the wooden building. Caleb held the reins of the horse-drawn cart as it rolled down the dusty road. The sun was just beginning to bow its head behind the horizon. Caniday sat next to him. "When we get to my ranch, it will be too late to show you what your work is, so I'll show you where you will sleep. Just do your work like you're supposed to and we will have no problems. But cross me and you will have hell to pay," Caleb instructed Caniday.

Caniday looked up at Caleb and nodded. He was tired and needed somewhere to stay the night—it might as well be there. He settled into the seat of the cart next to Caleb as they rode on. Caleb reached into his duffle bag and produced a slice of bread and handed it to Caniday. "Here, you must be hungry." Caniday grabbed the bread with both hands and greedily ate as they rode.

They arrived at Caleb's property, a sprawling ranch surrounded by a wooden fence that went on for miles. Caleb pulled up to a large ranch house and was greeted by a native ranch hand. "I'll take the horse, sir." The native spoke in English.

Caleb jumped down off the cart and, without acknowledging the ranch hand, motioned with his hand for Caniday to follow him. He led him to a tall barn structure that had straw spread out along the floor. Walking to the back of the barn, Caniday observed a pen just the size that a small calf would stand in.

"This is where you sleep," Caleb said as he held the pen door open for Caniday to enter. Bending down so as not to bump his head, he stepped into the pen. He turned to face the door that was shut and being locked with a padlock and held onto the wire cage as Caleb walked out of the barn.

"The foreman will come get you in the morning and show you your work." With that he shut the barn door, and in the dark Caniday lay down on the straw. Hunger gnawed at his stomach, and he missed his mama and grandfather. As he looked up through the moon-streaked slats of the roof of the barn, tears welled up in his eyes, filling them until a tear rolled down the side of his face and dripped into his ear.

The next morning, Caniday woke to the clanging of the padlock as it was being unlocked. "Come on outta there," a weathered and wrinkled face with a shaggy beard and gruff voice bark out at him. Caniday looked into the face of a tired old man with a checkered shirt and suspenders holding up his loose denim pants tucked into his worn leather boots. "I'm Ned. Here is your vittles" He handed him a bucket. "You can eat while I show you your duties. Caleb is a tough man but a fair one, so keep your nose clean and do what you are told to do and you won't have any trouble. Any questions?"

Shaking his head no, he looked into the pail of food that had been handed to him. It was a mixture of meat, peas, and corn. It had a funny smell, but he was so hungry he could eat a dead horse.

"You hear me, boy?" Ned scowled at him. "I better get an honest day's work outta you."

Caniday nodded his head, scooping up handfuls of the slop in the pail as they walked.

"Savages. I don't know why Caleb hires on your kind. You will start in the field. Have you ever used a hoe to get rid of weeds?" Ned asked.

"Uh huh," Caniday said in between mouthfuls of gruel.

"Okay then, this here's Solano." Ned pointed to a native man standing by the barn door. "He is an Injun like you. He grew up in the Missions, so he is an expert in field work. Follow him, and he will get you started." Caniday threw the empty pail down on the ground and proceeded to follow Solano out to the field, picking up a hoe along the way.

As they walked out to the field, Solano looked down at Caniday. "You are so young to be out on your own. What tribe are you? Why are you wandering alone?"

He looked up at Solano. "White men took my mama. I am looking for her," Caniday said as he examined the hoe in his hands.

"I hope you find her," Solano answered, looking skeptically at Caniday. "Here is all you need to do—we will start you off light until you get used to the work."

He started to dig up weeds the way he was shown. Solano walked away. After a few minutes, he grew bored. He found a caterpillar on a corn leaf and picked it up. He spent the rest of the day playing with it.

The days that followed were the same boring field work that Caniday was not used to. He would go into the field and sleep or run among the tall cornstalks, playing.

The second week of working on Caleb's ranch, instead of going to the field with Solano, Caleb unlocked the pen and ordered Caniday to get up into the cart, which was waiting outside the barn. "I knew it was a waste of money to buy you," Caleb said as he snapped the reins, making the horse go into a full gallop.

Caniday enjoyed the ride into town. They rode until Caleb stopped the cart in front of a tall wooden building that had piano music playing inside. Caleb got down from the cart. "C'mon, let's go," he said, pointing to the entrance of a saloon.

Caniday followed him inside the double swing doors. There inside were several tables and chairs with men sitting at them playing cards and drinking whiskey. A man was playing the piano, and there were several more men standing at the bar.

Caleb walked over to one of the tables with three men sitting at it and one empty chair. Sitting down, he greeted each man and put some dollar bills and some coins on the table. Caniday stood next to Caleb as he played a game of poker. They played several more hands. Caniday was getting restless and tried to wander off, only to be pulled back by Caleb with a jerk and an evil look. Another game and Caleb was down to his last coin.

A new game was about to start. Caleb spoke up. "I'm out. All I got left is this Injun I bought. A damn good little worker. Just like an ant he is—I will put him up for my ante, and taking a loss, I might add. Whoever wins the hand also wins the boy."

Caleb, a skilled poker player, purposely lost the next hand. "Well, Jonas," he said to the winner of the hand, "you got yourself a fine workhorse here. He's all yours." Caleb put his hat on and made a fast exit out the door, leaving Caniday standing near the table.

Jonas looked at Caniday. Realizing what had happened, he called after Caleb. "What am I gonna do with a boy? An Injun boy at that? I ain't got no use for one." He jumped up and ran out the swinging doors after Caleb.

Caniday, standing at the table, watched the two men leave the room. He looked around wondering what to do.

LUNA

Sore from riding side sideways on the horse of the man who stole her, Luna began kicking and flaying her arms. The man who took her stopped and pulled her upright to a sitting position in front of him. There was no escaping—her hands were tied to the saddle.

Her captors were talking and laughing as they rode, and Luna could not understand what they were saying. She could tell they spoke English, as she had learned a few words from the trappers who used to come through the village.

They rode for most of the day and finally stopped by a river. The man who held her got off his horse and picked her up by the waist to set her on the ground. "Why, when we clean you up, you ain't such a bad looker. My name's Tom, and this here's Nathaniel." He led her to a tree and secured her hands to a branch with a rope. Tom turned and joined Nathaniel in setting up a camp for the night.

Luna curled up next to the tree and tried the rope that held her. She pulled and tugged at it to see if she could escape, to no avail. Like a frightened animal caught in a trap, she kept her eyes on the two men sitting around the fire pit passing a bottle of whiskey back and forth until it was empty and Tom threw it against a rock.

Luna, half dozing, jumped at the shattering of the bottle. She shifted her weight and tried to find a comfortable position. Looking up, she saw Tom staggering toward her, unfastening his belted pants.

Fright overtook her discomfort and she pushed back against the tree to try to get away. "No! No!" Luna screamed as she kicked her foot toward the approaching Tom. He caught her leg in midstride and pulled her forward, her head hitting the ground with a thud. Falling on top of her now, he held her tied hands with one hand, at the same time forcing one knee between her legs and then the other one. His free hand found the knife in his belt, and with one stroke he cut her tunic up the front, exposing her naked body. Adjusting himself on top, he plunged himself inside her. The hot pain made her cry out, but he did not care. His free hand began stroking her body as she tried to kick him off. She tried to struggle free, but his weight was too much and she gave in. She could smell the whiskey and stale breath as he panted and grunted. She was filled with disgust as he finished his dirty deed and let out a final sigh indicating completion. "This here little squaw is gonna make us rich!" Tom said to Nathaniel as he pulled up his pants.

Luna, defeated, lay still as Nathaniel approached the compliant Luna unbuckling his belt. "I'll be the judge of that," he said as he mounted Luna.

When Nathaniel was done, he grabbed a blanket and tossed it to Luna. "Get some sleep. We have a long day of riding tomorrow. We are going to the gold mines!"

Luna took the blanket and wrapped it around her exposed body. Taking his place back at the campfire, Nathaniel scooped a tin of beans and offered it to Luna, who refused to eat. "Here eat this, you need to stay strong—we have big plans for you. You are gonna make us rich."

Luna turned away, facing the tree and holding her knees to her chest. There she sat through the night, crying for the loss of her family and her uncertainty.

LUNA

Joe and Nathaniel drove the wagon that held Luna and the supplies the mines to set up a camp. They chose to go up the Calaveras River. Luna, full of despair, rode in the wagon with her hands tied to it.

After a ride that seemed like it would never end, they reached an encampment dotted with little canvas tents along the riverbank. Stopping in the center of the encampment, Joe approached some miners bending down busily at the task of seeking gold who did not acknowledge him.

"Hey, fellas," Joe interjected. "I would like to take this opportunity to present to you a heaven on earth real life lady of the evening for your pleasure."

Nathaniel untied Luna and pulled her out of the wagon. Resisting, she pulled at the grip he had on her arm. Standing behind her, he put his hands on her shoulders and pushed her toward the miners. Luna stood there looking down at the ground. "Here she is, gents!"

This caught their attention, and they stood up. One miner looked up at Luna and then at Nathaniel and Joe. "Why, you soma bitch! We got a lady in this here camp already, and I mean a *lady*. She is given the respect due a *real* lady, not a common whore. Especially an Injun to boot. Why I wouldn't touch a filthy savage with a ten-foot pole. Now git in that wagon and skedaddle before I come up there and give you what for. I said *git!*"

Puzzled, Joe looked at the miner and then at Nathaniel, who shrugged his shoulders. They both turned back toward the wagon, and Nathaniel, holding Luna's hand, began to run to the wagon. He grabbed her about the hips and hoisted her up into the wagon as a rock hurled by Joe's head. Then another rock whizzed by and a hail of rocks rained down on him—he too ran to the wagon and jumped in as it sped off.

CANIDAY

Rosie, a prostitute who worked at the saloon that Caniday was abandoned in, witnessed the whole sham of a poker game that had been played by Caleb. She walked over to where the young boy was still standing.

"What's your name, honey?" she asked Caniday.

He looked up at her. She was tall and thin with blond hair and had lips painted bright red.

"I am Caniday. Mama said it is a strong name. Named after the coyotes howling the night I was born. I'm looking for my mama."

"Well, Caniday, come with me." She walked over to the bar-keep, a large-bellied man with red cheeks and thin, slicked-back hair. He was chewing on a cigar and wiping the bar with a folded towel. "Sam, we got this boy here. It seems he's been dumped on us. Can you put him to work?"

The bartender looked at Caniday and then at Rosie. "Jeez, Rosie, what am I running here? A home for orphans?"

Rosie looked at Sam and batted her eyelashes at him. He could never resist that beautiful face.

"Okay, I guess I could use some help around here. He can work for his food, and he can stay in the storeroom."

"Okay, kid, you can start by emptying those spittoons, and any time you see them full you empty them. Got it?"

Caniday hopped to it, grabbing the full pot that was at one end of the bar on the floor. Being careful not to spill its contents, he walked outside with it, returning a few minutes later with an empty pot.

"Now you go upstairs and empty those chamber pots," Sam said as he pointed to the rooms above the bar.

Rosie took Caniday by the hand, showed him where to find the pots, walked him out the back door, and showed him where to empty them. He emptied those pots until late into the night. When the saloon saw the last customer out, Sam found a sleeping Caniday behind the stairwell. He picked him up and set him down in the storeroom on some burlap sacks that were stacked there.

Routine days at the saloon for Caniday consisted of emptying chamber pots and spittoons and fetching breakfasts for guests and supper for Sam and Rosie. He took a liking to Rosie. She always left food on her plate for him; if not for her he would not eat. She was so pretty and was good to him…like his mama. He did not like that she had so many men friends, she always left upstairs with them when they came to the saloon.

The nights at the saloon were not so routine. The miners would pour in from the mines. They got drunk and played card games and got into fights. Drunken brawls were the norm, and they usually ended with fists flying and the participants being thrown out into the street to continue their beef.

One very warm night, the moon was so full it looked like you could touch it. A group of sailors came into the saloon. "Hey, mate," one said to Sam. "Your best whiskey for me and the gents and keep em coming!"

Sam looked at the man. "Say, where you gents from?"

"We're from the Land Down Under, Australia mate. We just got released from the penal colony. They shipped us here, and we are gonna try to strike it rich at the gold mines. Looking to have us a good time now that we landed in this good ole country of yours.

They started a heavy night of drinking and dancing and drinking some more. Rosie was doing a good job of keeping them entertained. They all took turns dancing with Rosie, until the Australians started to argue about who Rosie would go upstairs with. One of them stepped up on the first step, blocking the path of Rosie and another Australian.

"Here now, you're not taking the lady away just yet. We've just begun dancing!" said one to the other, and he pulled Rosie by the arm toward the others on the dance floor. This enraged the fellow, and he pulled Rosie's arm back toward him.

Rosie broke free, and the Australians took to brawling. Knives were pulled out of their boots and the fight became serious. The men were slashing at each other, weaving and bobbing, and the fight continued as the fellow mates at the bar laughed at the sight. The other men at the saloon jumped up from the tables to give the fighters some room. The piano player stopped. Rosie ran behind the bar. Sam pulled out a shotgun and shot a round into the air. The two fighters stopped and looked at Sam, his rifle still smoking.

"You boys take that outside. In fact, all you hooligans get out of my saloon! *Out!* Before you find out about Wild West justice," Sam shouted with a cigar dangling out of the corner of his mouth. "I said *beat it!*"

The group of Australians grumbled, gathered up their hats, put away their knives, and staggered out the door. "This here's not the only saloon in town!" one of them shouted as they left.

"Hey, kid," Sam said to Caniday as he threw a wet towel at him. "Wipe up the blood on the floor."

Caniday pulled the wet towel off his face, got on his hands and knees, and began mopping up the bloodied spots on the floor. The piano man went back to playing, and the gamblers sat back down at the tables. Rosie stepped over Caniday and, batting her eyelashes at the wealthiest player in the house, walked over and stood behind him. "Barkeep, champagne for the lady and a round for the house on me!" said the wealthy patron who had caught Rosie's attention.

Cries of joy filled the air in the saloon.

LUNA

Joe drove the wagon with Luna tied to the back for a few miles down along the edge of the river. He stopped when he reached the next encampment. This time, Nathaniel did the talking. He walked up to a man in a suit and top hat. The man was peering down on several men knee deep in the river with pans in their hands. The suited man turned to Nathaniel.

"Well, good day, sir," the suited man said. "What brings you to my establishment?" He pointed his cane to the several men panning for gold in the river below.

"I…we…" he stammered, looking at Joe sitting in the wagon and then back at the suited man, "have come to your fine camp sell here to sell our wares."

"I'm always looking for a business proposition. What, may I ask, are your wares?" the suited man asked as he gazed up at the beautiful Luna sitting demurely in the wagon.

"We have come to your fine camp for the lonely miner to get some female comfort. If only for a short time. We will set up our tent and for five minutes of pure heaven any man in your camp can have the pleasure, and I mean pleasure, of the company of this young creature…for a price," Nathaniel boasted.

"Well, now." The suited man walked up to the wagon and put his hand on Luna's chin, lifting up her face, looking into her eyes—into her very soul. He saw the sadness there, but he was a businessman and a greedy one at that. He said, "Very pretty and young. I think we can do business together for, let's say, fifty percent of the take."

"Fifty percent?" Joe stammered. "Why, this is our establishment, fifty percent is an outrage!"

Nathaniel walked over to Joe, still sitting in the wagon. "If we could talk him down to ten percent, I think we should take it," Nathaniel whispered.

"Ten," Joe said to the suited man.

"Thirty," said the man.

"Twenty and not a penny more," cried Joe.

"Okay, you have a deal. The name's York. You set up in my camp for twenty percent of the profit to me," chimed York.

"Shake on it, Mr. York. This here's Nathaniel and I'm Joe. This could be the beginning of a very profitable enterprise. The oldest profession right here in the mining camps! Whoo hoo!"

Joe and Nathaniel got to work setting up a tent with a cot and tied Luna's hands to it. Joe found a piece of discarded wood and fashioned a sign with the hours of business written in mud. The mining of the river stopped at dusk and resumed at first light of morning. The business hours were all night in between those hours.

"Open for business at sunset," Joe said to Nathaniel. "We is about to be very rich, my friend."

The air was cool in the wee hours of the night as Caniday stepped out of the saloon. The brightness of the full moon lit up the road that led out of town, and he decided to take it. Leaving the noise of the town behind him, he wandered into the open range.

Not knowing which direction to take, he spun around in a circle. He could see the lights of the distant Rancherias that dotted the countryside. He chose one and headed toward it. He was hungry, and settling the rumbling in his stomach was the only thought on his mind.

After walking for what seemed like hours, he came to a large house. It was the tallest building he had ever seen. He crept up to an open window and peeked inside. There was a dim light coming from the fire in the fireplace. The sound of crickets chirping was the only sound in the still night. Listening for any sign of life, he slipped into the open window. As his eyes adjusted to the light of the glowing embers, he looked around the large room. On a table, he found a bowl of grapes and apples and a wedge of bread. He stood at the table eating handfuls of grapes and walked around the room eating an apple. Something shiny caught his attention, and he tiptoed to it.

On the table up against the wall was a glass statue of a horse. He stared at it and stroked it with his fingers. It was smooth, and it felt cool on his skin. He held it up to the firelight and saw amazing rays of color and light. This was the most beautiful thing he had ever seen.

From the staircase, he heard a man's voice yelling up to someone as he walked down the stairs.

"I'll throw a couple more logs on the fire. That should hold until morning."

Caniday startled, set the glass statue quickly but quietly back in its place, and ran to the open window. He jumped out as the man of the house entered the room. "Who left the window open?" he asked out loud to no one as he walked to the open window and shut it.

Caniday landed in the dirt outside the window. He leaned up against the wall of the house and held his breath as the window was being shut just above his head. Then he jumped up and ran as fast as he could, his heart thumping in his chest.

A safe distance away from the house, he started walking back toward town. The night was showing its age, and fatigue overtook him. Along the road was an abandoned wagon with only three wheels. It wobbled as he climbed into it. He lay down and looked up at the fading stars. Curling up with his hand tucked between his legs, he fell fast asleep.

LUNA

Luna's first customer was a burly, greasy man with thick coat of hair on his back. Bristly with a week's worth of growth, his chin scratched and chafed her face. The man stunk of whiskey and filth, and she had to face away from him to keep from vomiting. He mounted the unwilling Luna and grunted and grinded for a short time—too long as far as Luna was concerned. There was a long line of men waiting their turn, and this went on through the night. By morning, Luna was exhausted and sore. She got up in the morning and was allowed to go the river. She pushed past the men who were mining there, not caring that one of the men fell into the water. She went in waist high to soothe her aching body. The thought of escape entered her mind. But where would she go? What direction would she take? She was exhausted. She would think about it after she rested.

Joe and Nathaniel were pleased at the profit they had made. Their greed was the only thing they cared about.

"Joe, my friend, at two dollars a pop, we will be swimming in dough!" Nathaniel chimed. That night, there was once again a long line in front of the tent that imprisoned Luna. Once again, she endured a night of dirty, smelly men grunting and grinding on top of her.

The next night, strangely, there was no line at Luna's tent. Joe, wondering what was happening to their business, went to Mr. York's tent. "Say, Mr. York, there's nobody coming for business. What's happening?"

Mr. York put his hand in his pocket and leaned on his cane. "Well, gentlemen, you see, it's like this. I took your idea and decided to go into business for myself. I recruited some of my own girls to entertain these hard-working gentlemen up here in the mines. My girls are American. You know, some of the men complained that they didn't much like being with a filthy squaw. Besides, they complained that she just laid there. They want action, and I aim to give it to them. Oh, and by the way, you still owe me the twenty percent of last night's take."

This infuriated Joe, while Nathaniel held onto his arm to keep him from taking a swing at Mr. York.

"Come on, Nate, let's get outta here. I don't like the company." With that, Joe and Nathaniel walked away, hitched up their horse to their wagon, and drove off, leaving Luna tied to her cot in her tent.

Mr. York went to Luna's tent. "I don't know if you can understand my language," he said. She nodded yes. "You now work for me. You will not be a prisoner any longer." He bent down and picked up the leather strap tied to Luna's leg and with a stroke of the knife in his belt she was cut free.

She rubbed her ankle where the leather strap had bound her to the cot. She looked up at him and smiled. He left the tent and returned a few minutes later with some dried meat and corn mush.

She hungrily took the bowl of food. As she ate, Mr. York explained to her how it was going to be.

"You now work for me. You will get a day off and food and this shelter. But you will work. I'll not have anyone slacking around here. You will still pleasure the men folk and do it right. You will service the men who line up outside your tent. Got it?"

She nodded her head and continued eating.

Caniday kept busy sweeping the floor of the saloon and emptying the spittoons and chamber pots. At night, the saloon was busy with gold miners spending their hard-earned diggings from the day. Monte and poker were the favorite games played. Long into the night, the miners drank whisky and gambled. Rosie stayed busy too, keeping the clients happy.

The English that he had learned from the trappers at the village came in handy. He would sweep and listen to the miners tell stories of the day's activities at the mines.

One night, a miner came into the saloon. He was not one of the regulars. As he sat at one of the Monte tables, Caniday overheard him bragging about a squaw that had been captured and was now living at the mines.

"There's this here squaw at the mines that was captured and is now a soiled dove for the miners—for two dollars you get five minutes with her," the miner boasted to the men at his table. "Uh huh, two fellers catched her, and now she works for them."

"Deal the cards, Johnnie," one of the gamblers at the table said.

"So for two dollars you can be with her for five minutes?" another miner asked. "I'll have to see about when I get up there tomorrow."

LUNA

That night, Luna did not work. Mr. York had brought in two prostitutes, Molly and Lilly, whom he had known from a business he owned in Wyoming but had gotten run out of town. They had long lines at their shared tent, and Luna was very happy to not have to work. She stood outside her tent, and for the first time she could see the sights that until now had just been images in her own imagination from the sounds of camp life…the images that she had thought of as she let her mind escape from her body as she lay in her cot with a client.

The smell of the campfires that dotted the encampment reminded her of her home village with her father and her son Caniday. How she missed her little boy. She thought about how her father would feel shame for her at what she was doing now.

She looked around at the campfires and watched groups of men, some drinking whiskey, some laughing, and some dancing. A card game here and an argument there. Such was camp life in the gold mines.

She returned to her tent and lay down on her cot, saddened at what her life had become, starting with the loss of her father and child.

It was the end of another day for Caniday. He sat outside the doorway of the saloon on the wooden planked walkway that lined the business district in the town of Stockton. The drunken patrons stumbled out after a night of drinking and gambling, leaving nothing in their pockets to show for the day's mining.

Caniday watched one drunken miner stumble out of the saloon and fall off the walkway, planting his face in the dirt. Just then, a wagon came speeding down the street and was about to run the drunk over. Caniday rushed into the street, grabbed the feet of the passed-out drunk, and pulled him out of the path of the wagon. As he did this, he saw the glint of a shiny object fall out of the pocket of the trousers of the passed out drunk.

Caniday looked around and, not seeing anyone, picked up the shiny object and put it in his waistband. Walking very swiftly, he went behind the saloon and hunched down between some wooden crates. Looking from side to side, he reached for the object and held it in his stretched-out hand. To his amazement, it was a gold nugget—a fairly large one that filled the small palm of his hand. He was elated. Suddenly his mind was dancing with the thoughts of what he would do with this newfound bonanza. Too excited now to sleep, he started walking out of town toward the ranch that held the glass horse.

LUNA

The nights were busy in the mines, filled with lines of clients for Molly and Lilly, as they were good at their line of work and the men loved them. Not so for Luna; her clients diminished to the point that Mr. York was getting concerned, because she was becoming a burden to him.

One day, Mr. York took Molly and Lilly to Stockton for supplies. The camp was quiet with the miners at their claims. Luna watched them ride off.

She entered the tent that Molly and Lilly shared. It was much larger and elegantly done. It had silken linens on the cots lined with several soft pillows. A boudoir cabinet with rows of colorful silken robes and corsets, several pairs of heeled shoes, and many scarves. So many beautiful scarves, the like of which she had never seen before. She stroked them and felt the material glide through her fingers.

There was a wash stand with a basin full of lilac water, and on a table there were rows of perfumes. She picked one up, feeling the glass in her hand and taking a big sniff of it. She liked the smell. Then her eye caught a blond wig with ringlets and a looking glass. She picked up the looking glass and gazed upon herself, turning her head from left to right and back again. She had seen her reflection in the pond at her village, but this was different. "I am beautiful," she said out loud. She picked up the blond wig and put it on her head. The wig sat on top of her head slightly askew, and she giggled in the looking glass. Taking off the wig, she went back to the brightly colored scarves.

There were so many of them, and they were so beautiful; she selected one and put it around her neck. She went back to the looking glass as she admired herself. "They have so many; they won't miss this one," she said to her image in the looking glass, and she walked back to her tent to hide her ill-gotten treasure under her pillow.

Mr. York and the ladies arrived back to camp by early evening. Molly and Lilly were loaded up with packages and bundles. They quickly went into their tent to get ready for the night's business.

Mr. York entered Luna's tent with a package tied up with a string. Luna was sitting on her cot mending a hole in her tunic. She looked up at Mr. York as he entered her tent.

"Luna, my dear, I have a gift for you." Mr. York handed the package to Luna.

Setting her tunic aside, Luna pulled the string on the package to display a gown of the most beautiful red silk she had ever seen. It was even prettier than the ones in Molly and Lilly's tent. She stood up and held it up to her.

Along with the gown was a lacy corset of pink and white. "Now you can feel as beautiful as you look," said Mr. York.

With that, Mr. York walked out. Holding the gown up to her, Luna danced around the tent as much as the cramped space would allow. That night, she wore the gown, and she did feel beautiful. She had a few more clients than the previous nights.

The next morning, Luna woke up to hear Molly's loud voice from the tent she shared with Lilly. She was carrying on about something Luna could not understand.

All at once, Molly came bursting into Luna's tent. Her face was red and her eyes were bulging. "You!" She pointed her finger in Luna's face. "You have been in my things! I am missing a scarf—my favorite one! You stole it from me!" Molly stood over Luna with her hands on her hips.

"I don't know what you are talking about. I didn't steal anything," Luna stammered as she pushed the stolen scarf farther under her pillow.

Molly stood over her for a minute, staring down at her. Then, in a flash, she was next to Luna's cot, grabbing it and flipping it over. Luna went flying and landed, with arms flailing, on the dirt floor. With the cot tipped over, the scarf was exposed. Both ladies froze and stared at it. Molly bent down and snatched it up. Shaking it in Luna's face, she shouted, "I knew it! You filthy, lying savage!"

Luna jumped up and slapped Molly in the face.

For an instant, Molly stood in shock at this bold move. Then rage overcame her and she lunged at Luna, both hands grabbing hands full of Luna's hair. Luna managed to grab both of Molly's legs and pull them out from under her. Molly landed flat on her ass, letting go of Luna's hair.

Just then Lilly showed up at the entrance to the tent. "What's going on in here?" she asked with a smirk on her face.

"This thieving Indian squaw stole my scarf! I found it here!" She pointed to the toppled cot and bedding.

"Well, honey, if you wanted to borrow a scarf, all you had to do was ask," Lilly said. "I would have let cha." Lilly turned to leave Luna's tent. "Come on, Moll, it ain't worth it; we gals gotta stick together in this hellhole till we make enough dough to make a better life."

Molly got up with the scarf in hand. As she got near the tent Mr. York came running up from the river when he heard the commotion. He grabbed Molly by the waist and pushed her to one side. He pulled Luna by the hand on one side and Molly by his other hand, looking back and forth at the two ladies. "Now, ladies, I can't have fighting among you. Whatever it is that's got you two in an uproar, please settle it right now!"

"She stole my scarf!" shouted Molly indignantly.

Mr. York let go of Molly's hand. "Get back to your tent—I'll handle this! *Now!*" he shouted. With that, Molly walked back to her tent.

"Now then, Luna, is this true? After I took you in when those two idiots left you? I cannot tolerate thievery. I will not tolerate it!"

Luna shamed, looked to the ground. "It was only one scarf. She has many, and they are so beautiful," Luna said with a quivering voice.

Mr. York, stepping lively, entered Luna's tent. He came out with the red gown he had given her the day before. He took a knife from its sheath on his belt. With a stroke of the knife, he cut the gown. Putting the knife back, he ripped the gown in two and threw it into Luna's tent. Next he got a piece of wood that was sitting in the campfire. With the end of the wood ablaze, he threw it into Luna's tent. The fire rapidly turned into an inferno, and the little canvas tent was destroyed.

Luna watched in horror as all she owned was gone. Mr. York charged toward Luna. Picking her up, he tossed her over his shoulder, walked to the edge of the river, and threw her in. The river, swollen by recent rains, rolled with rapids of great speed and carried Luna with it.

Luna struggled to stay afloat, arms flailing in the violent currents. Losing strength and growing exhausted trying to fight to stay above the water, Luna eventually began sinking. She did not know how far she had gone downstream. With her head underwater, she tried to grab hold of a hanging tree branch on the riverbank. In desperation, her only hope was to keep one arm raised above the water line in an attempt to grab one.

As she ran out of her last breath, she tumbled and rolled downstream with the rapid waters. Her lungs began burning with spasms for air. In her mind, the only thought was that she was about to die.

Then she felt a hand on her arm and she was yanked up out of the water. Gasping, choking, and spitting, she gulped in the delicious air.

"You okay, little lady?" she heard a man voice ask.

Looking up into the face of an angel, she smiled.

CANIDAY

Waking up the next morning, before he even opened his eyes, Caniday felt for the nugget to make sure it wasn't just a dream. Verifying that it wasn't, he smiled and sat up. He had fallen fast asleep in the field on the outskirts of town in a pit that he had covered with dead tumbleweeds, being careful not to stick himself on the sharp thorns. As he walked, he thought of what he would do with his newfound wealth.

He decided that he needed a pair of boots. Boots that would keep his feet warm and dry this coming winter. Leather ones with silver trim. Now he had to figure out a way to purchase these. He he thought about the new boots he would buy. He had never owned anything like them. He daydreamed about them all day—what they would look like and what they would feel like. He could not buy the boots himself, because he knew that native people were cheated and swindled when they purchased goods at the general store. He had to find someone he could trust to buy them for him.

Leaving the field he reached the edge of town. He walked down the middle of the dirt street that was the business district of Stockton.

He walked by the general store, past the ice house, and past another saloon. The assay office across the street had a line of men waiting to weigh their panning take for the day. He could see the port at the end of the street. Walking past the sheriff's office/ jailhouse, he saw the drunk man who had lost the nugget. He and the sheriff were outside the jailhouse. The drunk was talking very loudly to the sheriff.

"Someone stole it right out of my pocket!" he cried.

"Well now," said the sheriff, "you can't identify anyone in particular to point your finger at. That is what you get for getting falling down drunk. Unless you can come up with a witness, I can't help ya."

"But, sheriff, I—" He stopped talking as both men turned to stare at Caniday as he walked by.

Caniday kept right on, not altering his speed, and then after he passed them he walked at a slightly faster pace. Past the theater, the firehouse, another saloon, the blacksmith…all the way to the end of the street at the entrance to the port. If he kept walking, he would end up at the State Insane Asylum just outside of town. There was no one he could trust.

He ran back to the saloon where he worked. There was a bigger crowd than usual tonight. More miners drinking, gambling, fighting, and even dancing with each other. There had been a big bonanza in the mines earlier that day, and the men from that mine were celebrating big.

"Drinks are on me!" and "This round is on me!" were heard throughout the evening. It was one of the wildest nights Caniday had seen at the saloon.

The fights at the saloon started early that night too, when one of the gamblers accused another of cheating at cards, fueled by too much whiskey. Fists were flying and tables were being overturned. Rosie screamed and ran. People were running for the safety of the overturned tables and behind the bar. The piano music stopped.

Sam reached for his shotgun and fired a round into the air. Everybody stopped in their tracks and looked at Sam.

"Take it outside, or I'll settle it with this here shotgun!" shouted Sam.

The fighting men, grumbling and picking up their hats from the floor, stumbled out and disappeared into the chilly night.

The saloon patrons went back to drinking and gambling, and the piano music resumed playing a dance tune.

Caniday was standing next to the saloon door when he heard the glass shatter and saw the explosion of flames burst into life as the whiskey bottle with a flaming rag hit the saloon floor. Caniday ran out. The saloon patrons scattered into many directions in an attempt to vacate the room with the spreading inferno. Sam ran out and down the street to the firehouse.

Several people came running with buckets and pails in hand. The fire brigade arrived, led by Sam. A long line of volunteers passed buckets of water hand to hand from the port to the saloon, but they made little to no progress.

A gust of wind whipped up the flames at an alarming rate, sending cinders flying to nearby structures and canvas tents. Soon the whole business district was ablaze. People were rushing out of burning buildings and into the streets, helplessly watching their town burn to the ground.

In the morning, Caniday walked the street to assess the damage. The damage was great. He found Sam sitting on the street outside of where his saloon had been; it was now replaced by smoldering ash and charred wood.

"Well, little fella, what do you think?" Sam asked him. Caniday just stood next to him without saying a word.

"I could go to the mines and do some panning, I reckon. I always wanted to strike it rich. I'll get some supplies together and head up to the mines," Sam said.

Caniday put his hand in his waistband where the gold nugget was tucked away. "Can you buy me some boots?" he asked Sam.

Sam looked at him with a hearty laugh that shook his fat belly and asked, "How do you think to pay for these boots?" Sam asked with the cigar dangling from his lips.

Caniday pulled the nugget out of the waistband of his pants. He held it up to Sam. Sam's eyes got as big as saucers at the sight of the gold nugget in the boy's hand. He took the nugget and held it up to the light. "Well, I'll be, where did you get this?"

Caniday just stood silent.

"Sure, I can get you some boots with this. I'll get you the finest boots this here nugget'll buy. Meet me here tonight, and I'll have your boots waiting for you. Sure thing. I'll do that very thing," Sam said as he rose to his feet.

Caniday sat down as Sam walked off. The morning sun felt good on his face. By afternoon, as the sun started to set, the anticipation was getting the best of him. Any minute, Sam would be here with his new boots. By nightfall, he was looking up and down the street but there was no sign of Sam. He started walking up and down the street, and soon he was running up and down the deserted street of burned out buildings and tents.

He saw Rosie up ahead going into a saloon down the street that had survived the fire. It was packed with miners drinking whiskey and gambling. The place was much more crowded than Sam's ever was, because all but this one had burned down.

Caniday ran into the saloon. "Rosie!" he shouted after her.

"Whoooaaa! You cain't come in here, sonny," said the waiter as he wiped a table near the entrance.

Rosie appeared at the doorway. "Oh, let him in. He's harmless as a fly," she said to the waiter as she opened one swinging door to let him in.

What's up, kid?" she asked.

"Rosie, have you seen Sam? He was supposed to meet me at sundown," Caniday asked with desperation.

Rosie put her hand on his shoulder and, looking down into his distressed face, she said, "Why, yes I did see him. He was at the assayer's office cashing in some gold that he had, and then he said he was leaving on the next stage out of here. He didn't say where to, but he's long gone, honey, he left town on the afternoon stage."

Caniday stood staring in disbelief. He walked out without saying a word and started walking down the street with his head hung down. He walked out into the outskirts of town into the field until he got to the ranch with the glass horse. Not seeing anyone around, he slipped in through an open window.

Finding some food to eat, he sat down next to the table eating and holding the glass horse up to the light of a gas lamp.

After he filled up on grapes, apples, and bread, he headed back to town. Not knowing where he would sleep, since the saloon was gone, he found the dirt pit and made himself a bed covered with tumbleweeds for the night. He could hear the howling of the coyotes in the distance, and it was comforting to him as he fell asleep thinking of his mama.

LUNA

The bearded man pulled Luna the rest of the way out of the water onto the shore. He ran to his camp gear and grabbed a blanket to wrap around the shivering Luna.

"You need to get out of those wet clothes. Go behind those bushes yonder and take them off. Here are some dry clothes to wear while they dry." He handed her a pair of woolen trousers and a red checkered cotton shirt. "Put these on. Then hand me your wet things and I'll put them next to the fire to dry."

She stood up on wobbly legs and did as instructed. Then she sat near the fire and savored the warmth of it.

"Now then, what's your name, little lady? I am John Saxby. You can call me Jaxby. Pleased to make your acquaintance."

"I'm Luna," she said shyly.

"Well, Luna darling, I am a trapper. I was just about to fix some grub. You hungry?"

She nodded her head and smiled.

Jaxby treated her like a gentleman treats a lady, not knowing her recent past, and she wasn't about to tell him.

They spent the next winter in the Central Valley of California, snuggled up in a little wooden cabin he had built. In the spring, they traveled up to the Sierras and beyond. They went up the Oregon Trail to the Lassen Mountains and Shasta Mountains, and beyond into the Northern Territories, where they stayed with the local native tribes. Then in the fall, they headed back down to Mount Diablo.

Jaxby collected many firs and skins—enough to line his purse when sold to the trading company and for her to make them both functional clothing.

The following winter, as they settled into their little wooden cabin, Luna discovered that she was pregnant. This was the happiest time of her life. Jaxby was happy to have a woman to warm him through the winter, cook his meals, and mend his clothing...and now to give him a child.

By spring, Luna was big with child, and when the day of the birth came, she went out into the forest as she had done with the birth of Caniday. Her labor came fast and strong. Squatting on a bed of pine needles, she gave one last push, and the baby slid out. She looked down with love at what she had created. The baby boy looked just like Caniday had at his birth, but what should have been great joy turned surreal. The baby boy was a deep shade of blue and was not breathing. She picked up his little body and gently shook him. She set him down and pushed at his chest, all to no avail. She lay the motionless body down as the tears welled up in her eyes. She picked him up and, holding him close to her chest, she wailed a death cry that filled the valley.

Jaxby kept busy all that long night with anticipation of meeting his child. By morning, Luna came back to the wooden cabin. She was holding her bundle wrapped in a blanket with no joy. She cried as she held her baby close to her body, fell to her knees at Jaxby's feet, and wept. Jaxby gently put his arms on her arms and pulled her up, holding her close. Between sobs she stammered, "My love, our baby died—he died because of me!"

"How so? What did you do to cause the child's death? What did you do, Luna?" he asked, first puzzled and then demanding.

"I am being punished. I was stolen from my village by two white men. I was taken to the gold mines. I had to be with many men. I had to sell my body for these men for survival."

Jaxby pulled away from her. He took the lifeless bundle of baby, his baby, still wrapped in a blanket from her and walked out the door without saying anything.

The next day, while the rain poured down in sheets outside, Jaxby woke Luna up, wrapped her in a bearskin coat, pulled her outside with a bundle of her clothes, and put her up on a horse.

Getting on his horse, he held the reins that led her horse to Stockton, all without saying a word. When they reached town, the deep, muddied streets were empty. He slid off of his horse, stepping into a deep puddle of mud. He took the reins of Luna's horse and tied them to a hitching post outside of an abandoned building with the rain still pouring down. Without speaking, he got back on his horse and rode away.

Luna was devastated. "Jaxby! Jaxby! Don't leave me! I love you! Jaxby!" she cried, the tears mixing with the rain falling on her face.

CANIDAY

The rain was relentless as Caniday walked back to town after raiding the food storage at the ranch outside of town. The vast field between town and that ranch had once been lush and open and was now full of cattle and sheep. It lay barren, and fences blocked the freedom of his travels.

Arriving back in town, he went behind the building that housed the sheriff's office and the jail. There behind the building, he found some discarded canvas tarps and planks of wood left over from the rebuilding of the jailhouse that had burned down. He fashioned a shelter for himself, lining the ground with a scrap of canvas. He used one wall of the building and built the other walls out of what was remaining of the canvas and some wood scraps, taking care that it still looked like a pile of rubble so he would not be detected. It was dry and comfortable. He lay down and fell fast asleep, listening to the rhythm of the rain dancing on his tarp shelter.

Upon waking, he nibbled on some bread that he had stolen from the ranch he had just raided. He also took a small bite into a potato and an apple, carefully conserving his store of food. He peeked out into the bright sunlight reflecting off the puddles left by the rain.

The sound of men's voices captured his attention, and he realized that he could hear everything going on in the sheriff's office on the other side of the wooden wall of his shelter.

"Sheriff Dodd, I'm here to report a theft at my food storage shed," said a man's voice. "This is not the first time either! What are you going to do about it?"

"Well now, Colonel Jackson," the sheriff said in a calm tone. "What do you want me to do about it? You live outside of the town's boundaries and are therefore out of my jurisdiction.

Caniday listened as the two men talked on the other side of the wall. It was Colonel Jackson's voice he now recognized. He listened intently as the man complained about the food theft and quickly realized he himself was the thief.

"The facts are that someone is stealing my food stores, and I'm about to bring Mrs. Jackson home from the state asylum. She has been there six months now. It's time she came home, and I don't need a person or persons lurking about and scaring her. She is so delicate ever since our only son died in the war. I brought her out here and built her a beautiful home to live in to get her mind right again."

"I'm glad to hear your wife is doing better Colonel Jackson. But the fact remains that I can't help you." The sheriff stood with his thumbs hitched in his trouser pockets.

Just then gunshots rang out. "What in tarnation?" the sheriff said as he reached for his gun on his hip. There was silence for a moment, and then the door burst open and Caniday could hear the shuffling of feet entering the room.

"Sheriff Dodd! Come quick! There has been a robbery at the Bank of Stockton! The varmints took off with sacks of gold!" a frantic man's voice was heard shouting.

The sheriff started barking orders at his deputy. "Otis! Get the rifles, round up some men, and meet me outside! Colonel Jackson, I'm afraid this conversation will have to wait—I got pressing business here in town to attend to." With that, Caniday heard feet shuffling on the wooden floor and a door closing.

Caniday ran out of his makeshift shelter to the front of the building to watch the posse of men on horseback ride out of town. Colonel Jackson stepped out of the sheriff's office door and noticed Caniday standing in the street. He looked down his nose at him. With a snarl and a "Harrumph!" he crossed the street to the saloon.

Caniday wandered down the street to the port to watch the ships coming in with more immigrants, mostly men with tools and supplies heading for the gold mines.

He stood next to the plank as the arrivals disembarked and shouted to the passengers. "Need directions? For a small fee I know the best places to pan for gold! Need to know where to stay? For a small fee I can show you the best place in town. Need to buy supplies? For a small fee I can help there too." The steady stream of men passed him by without even a nod.

The last of the people walked off down the street. Caniday, disappointed that he was not noticed, started to walk away.

"Hey kid," a woman's voice sang out. "I need a place to stay. Will you carry my bag?"

Caniday turned to see a beautiful tall blonde. She had on a large blue hat that matched her very low-cut gown, and it had a feather on it that shaded her lily white face—a face with the brightest color of red on her lips that he had ever seen.

"Yes, ma'am, I can do that." Caniday picked up the bag the lady had set down. It was a little heavy but he managed. He directed her to the hotel just up the street from the port.

"This is the best place to stay," Caniday said as he set her bag down outside the hotel door. The lady smiled, reached into her velvet bag, and withdrew a dollar coin. She handed it to Caniday.

Elated, Caniday stared at it. He clenched it tightly and ran off to his shelter behind the sheriff's office.

No sooner had he settled into his shelter than he heard several footsteps and men shouting on the other side of the wall. It was Sheriff Dodd's voice that stood out, and he also heard the rattling of keys and the clanging of an iron door. "We got you red-handed. You make yourself comfortable in this here jail cell. I'll send for the circuit judge, and we will have a trial by next week. Enjoy your last days, because you'll be tried and hung for the killing of a citizen in the progress of a robbery. You are under arrest for murder and robbery." The cell door slammed shut with a sound that made Caniday jump with a start.

Several voices filled the room as the posse that had accompanied the sheriff was heard in protest.

"Sheriff, this varmint killed Bill Jenkins, the bank teller. There are witnesses. He is guilty as sin. I say we take him out and hang him right now!"

"Yeah, he broke the law. The Bible says an eye for an eye! Let's hang him!" The crowd of men in the Sheriff's office were all yelling at once for the man to be hung.

Caniday sat still in his shelter as the voices on the other side of the wall grew louder and more adamant. Then a gunshot was heard and the room fell silent.

"All of you, out. This is my jailhouse and I am the sheriff, and I say we follow the law. We wait for the judge and have a proper trial."

The sound of shuffling feet, grumbling men's voices, and a door being shut was heard.

"Otis, you stay here and guard the prisoner. I'm going to send Jacob to fetch the judge; we can't wait until next week, not with that angry crowd."

"Yes, sir'" Otis replied.

Before Sheriff Dodd could open the door to leave, he looked out the window "Oh, damn it. Here comes that nosy reporter for the newspaper. What's he doing in this town anyway?" Sheriff

Dodd flung open the door. "I'm very busy and don't have time to talk to you!"

"Now, you know it is the public's right to know. Who have you got in your jail cell? What is he charged with?" The reporter followed Sheriff Dodd out the door and followed him across the street to the saloon.

All the excitement of the bank robbery and the capture made Caniday hungry He decided to go to Colonel Jackson's ranch to raid his food stores and look at that glass horse statue once again. Caniday felt safe out on the open range, His grandfather taught him how to find good hiding places. He left town and began walking the trail that led to the ranch. He climbed up on top of a ridge, and as he approached the top he heard a peculiar sound that he had not heard before. Standing up high on the ridge, he strained his ears toward the sound. He looked to the east and could not believe his eyes.

A long line of horse-drawn wagons stretched as far as his eyes could see. Horses and cows, huddled in bunches, trailed the long line. Men on horseback cracked whips and whistled. Dogs ran to and fro, keeping the herds moving.

In his excitement, he ran toward the wagon train. When he was still some distance away, he heard a shot ring out and a puff of dirt landed just in front of his feet. He stopped dead in his tracks and looked at a man standing up on his wagon, pointing a shotgun at him.

"Not another step closer!" the man shouted.

Caniday stood in bewilderment.

"We don't want any trouble, but we will kill any Injun who tries to attack us!" the man with the shotgun yelled.

Caniday turned and ran back up the ridge. Hiding behind a bush, he watched the procession as it rode past. It took all of the afternoon to pass by headed toward town.

LUNA

She slid off of her horse, leaving it standing in the rain, and started walking, the mud oozing through her toes. Wandering aimlessly, she found herself standing in front of a saloon. She stepped up on the wooden platform and ventured through the swinging doors.

The room was alive with drinking, gambling, laughing men, with painted ladies dotting the scene in various poses with prospective clients.

Luna approached an open space at the bar. The saloon keeper, a robust man with more bushy hair on his face than on his head. "I'll have a whiskey," she said boldly.

The barkeep stopped drying a glass and turned toward the source of the request, his cigar nub hanging out of the corner of his mouth and singeing his beard. "What do we have here?" said the barkeep with a jiggle to his belly as he laughed. The crowd at the bar joined in on the laughter, and it resonated throughout the saloon. The next moment, the room fell silent.

Luna, undaunted, repeated her request and waited for the barkeeper's response. He slammed the glass down and placed the towel on the bar. Placing both hands on the bar, he looked Luna up and down. "We don't serve Injuns in this saloon, and I reckon you don't have any coin to pay even if we did. Now turn yourself around and git right outta here the same way you came in before I throw you out." He pointed toward the door. The room again broke out in a roar of laughter.

Luna stood and stared at the round, red face in front of her. She was about to turn and run when a gentle voice behind her spoke out. "Why, I'll buy the little lady a drink."

She spun around to look up at the dirt-covered, toothless grinning face of the gentle-voiced man. She smiled at him and nodded her head.

"I'll take a bottle of whiskey," he said as the jingling sound of coins hitting the bar rang out. The barkeeper reached under the bar, pulled up a bottle of whiskey, and set it on the bar. With one move, the gentle man reached around Luna, grabbed the bottle with his fur-covered arm, wrapped it around Luna, and led her out the swinging doors to the saloon.

Luna walked into the cool night air with the man's arm around her. He pulled the cork out of the bottle of whiskey with his mouth and took a swallow, grimacing as the firewater landed in his belly. With his arm still around Luna's shoulders, he escorted her to the side of the building, in an alleyway between the bar and the next building. He handed the bottle to Luna and, with his hands free, he nudged her against the wall of the building and began kissing her neck and caressing her breasts.

Luna took the bottle, put it up to her mouth, and took a big gulp of the amber liquid. It burned down her throat and down her chest, and it got even hotter in the pit of her stomach. She didn't notice or care that all the while the gentle man was lifting her dress with one hand and holding up one of her legs, placing his penis inside her. She took another gulp of the numbing goodness as the man plunged deeper into her body, thrusting his body—not so gently—in and out. The gentle man continued panting and groaning as she took another gulp of the whiskey, enabling her to feel nothing. Finally, with one last thrust he shuddered and, breathing heavily, stopped moving. He pulled himself away from her and, buttoning up his pants, he said, "Thank you, little lady. You can keep the bottle," as he walked away.

Luna straightened herself and her dress, still wet from the rain. She sat down on the dry ground of the alley and finished the bottle of whiskey.

After the long wagon train had passed by, Caniday ventured to the trail it had followed. Refuse littered the roadway. There were items scattered as far as he could see. He started walking and picking up various things. He grabbed a pot, examined it, and then tossed it aside. All afternoon, he picked through the rubble left behind by the newcomers, picking through wooden boxes of clothing and kitchenware, children's toys, and furniture. By late afternoon, he was bored with this and was about to abandon his game and go back to town when an overturned wagon caught his eye.

He crept up to the overturned wagon slowly, and got down on his hands and knees so he could peer inside. He saw the body of a young man. "Hey, mister, you sleeping?" he asked.

There was no response. Caniday reached in and gave the man a poke with his finger. The man did not move, so Caniday gave him a shove. Still no movement. He sat back and observed the man lying under the overturned wagon and determined that he must be dead. Looking at the body head to toe, He noticed that his booted feet were sticking out of the wagon covered by some rubble. Removing the rubble, he untied one boot and pulled it off the body. Examining it, he discovered it was not too worn. He put his foot in the boot. It was a little big, but he was so overjoyed at having boots he didn't mind. He unlaced the other boot and slipped it off the dead man's foot. Pulling the other boot off of his own foot, he held the boots close to his chest and started walking back toward town and the boxes of clothes he had seen earlier.

Finding a box with discarded shirts, he picked one up and tore it into cloth strips, which he stuffed into the toes of the boots, packing them tight. Next, he found some old woolen socks that were so large that the heel of the sock went halfway up his shin. Putting on the large socks and boots and tying the laces tight, he walked around in a circle and then stomped around, kicking up his heels. The boots stayed on his feet, and he was elated to finally have a pair of boots.

The sun was setting in the western sky, and it was getting chilly. He found a Sunday coat in the box of clothes. He put it on even though the sleeves covered his hands. Now he was set for winter. He walked back into town in his new attire.

The first thing Caniday wanted to do when he got back into town was to go to the hotel where Rosie was working and show her his new boots. When he got to the hotel, he was stopped at the door.

"No Injuns allowed, sonny, and specially no young'uns!" the doorman growled at him.

"I just want to show Rosie my new boots," Caniday pleaded with the doorman.

"Well she ain't here no more. Now run along before I throw you out into the street." The doorman waved his hand at him, shooing him like he would a pesky fly.

Not believing the burly doorman. Caniday needed to see for himself that she was gone. "But I need to see her!" Caniday said adamantly, pushing past him.

The doorman, caught off guard, took one step toward Caniday, grabbing him by the oversized coat at the scruff of the neck and pulling it off. Caniday bolted inside and ran up the stairs to where Rosie's room was.

The doorman stood there with both hands full of the coat that used to be on Caniday and growled with anger. He threw the coat to the floor and began running after him, but he had already reached Rosie's door. Bursting through the door, he ran inside and stopped short at the foot of the bed. There in the bed was a naked man lying on top of a naked woman, but the woman was not Rosie. The naked man jumped up, grabbed his gun out of the holster that was hanging on the bedstead, and pointed it at Caniday. The naked woman sat up on her knees with a squeal, her breasts swaying to and fro.

The doorman finally reached the door, huffing and puffing. "You little shit! I'm gonna kick your ass! Sorry, Bell, this boy runs as fast as a rabbit!"

Bell smiled at Caniday, not hiding her nakedness. "You are a little young to visit upstairs, little fella."

"Pete, get this runt outta here!" the naked man with the gun said as he used it to hide his private parts.

"I need to see Rosie," Caniday said, breathless from running up the stairs.

"Well she ain't here!" the man with the gun said as he climbed back into the bed, pulling a sheet over his trunk.

"She moved on to San Francisco, honey. She left a week ago," Bell said softly to Caniday.

Caniday, dejected, looked down at his boots. He turned around and looked up at the red-faced doorman.

Walking past the doorman, he felt a kick to his backside that sent him sailing through the air and rolling down the stairs. He landed at the bottom of the stairs in a room full of gamblers and drunks. The room fell so silent for a brief moment that you could hear a pin drop, and then it filled with the roar of laughter.

Caniday stood up and rubbed his rump as he walked out behind the saloon among the wooden boxes and trash. He squatted down with his back against the wall. There were some pebbles on the ground, and he picked one up and threw it as hard as he could at a tin bucket. Here he stayed until he fell asleep where he sat.

LUNA

Luna opened one eye. She sat up, leaning on the wall of the building. She looked around. She was still in the alley she had passed out in the night before. Her head ached and her stomach was on fire. She began to cough. It started out small, and then a deep cough wracked her whole body. She got onto her hands and knees, arching her back in an effort to stop the hacking. She felt like she would cough up her insides, as a splash of blood landed on the ground in front of her.

The coughing stopped. She sat back up to catch her breath and shivered as the cool morning air hit her sweat-drenched body. Standing up on wobbly legs, she felt dizzy and fell back onto the wall of the building.

The barkeep heard a thump on the wall of his building and went out to investigate. Peeking around the corner, he saw Luna. "Get outta here, you drunken whore! You give a place a bad name!"

Luna started walking, wandering away from the port past the dry goods, the livery stable, and the butchery.

She came up on a canvas shelter with a woman standing at the entrance. The woman smiled at Luna, holding out her arms in invitation. "Come in. All are welcome here. Come in—we have food for your body and your soul," the woman offered.

Luna decided to enter; it was a large room with tables and wooden benches, with men sitting here and there. There were more men standing in line with bowls and spoons in hand. At the front of the line was the woman who had called Luna inside. She stood next to a man scooping food from a large black kettle hanging over a fire. He placed a heaping ladle full of steaming meat stew into each man's empty bowl. The aroma filled the air. Luna could not remember the last time she had eaten. She was handed a bowl and spoon by a toothless bearded man in dirty rags. "Hi, I'm Joseph. I work here with the Jamesons."

Luna reached the front of the line. The woman smiled at her. "We don't see many women in here. In fact, I believe you're the first. Let us fill your bowl." A ladle of hot stew was placed in her bowl by Joseph. "Eat. Then we will sing hymns after. My name is Mabel Jameson. My husband and I are missionaries. We run this shelter along with our helper, Joseph."

Luna carried her bowl over to an empty table, sat down, and put a spoonful of the meat stew to her lips. It soothed her rumbling stomach, but after only eating a few bites she pushed the bowl away.

"Not hungry?" Mabel asked her. Luna shook her head. "I have an extra fur wrap I would like for you to have. I'll just be a minute." She returned with a shawl made of rabbit skin. "Here, this will keep you warm."

Pastor Jameson entered the canvas church and stood next to Mabel. "Well, here's my lovely wife. Who do we have here?"

Mabel smiled up at her husband. "We have our first woman participant." She looked down at Luna. "I do hope you will stay and hear our sermon tonight."

Luna did not answer. She remembered being a child in the Mission. She thought of her father, who had risked his life when he escaped with her from that place. She did not know if she could trust these people.

Pastor Jameson and Mabel went to the front of the tent. He stood behind the podium and, with Mabel by his side, began the sermon. "Let us pray."

Everyone bowed their heads. Luna slipped out the door.

She walked down to the port saloon. There she stood outside the door in the shadows and sold her body through the evening for the whiskey that made her not feel. She savored the numbness of drinking whiskey. Then it was back to the safety of the canvas church to sleep it off on a wooden bench.

Pastor Jameson noticed Luna sleeping in the church each morning. "Mabel, that poor lost soul. We must save her from herself. How can I get through to her to see the evil of her ways?"

"I don't know, dear, but for now we can gain her trust by letting her stay here nights until we do."

"She is a very ill woman; I have noticed a rash on her arms—advanced syphilis, I would guess—and her cough is the consumption. The poor wretch."

Mabel nodded her head in agreement.

The wagon train entering the town made a commotion that drew a crowd. Caniday fell in behind the train of wagons. They stopped at the Public House, where newcomers first stopped in the developing town. The proprietor, a short, thin man with greasy strands of gray hair resting on his shoulders, stepped out into the sunshine. Squinting, he placed his worn leather hat atop his head, and his belly jiggled between the suspenders that held up his brown woolen pants. He stepped to the head of the crowd in front of the wooden building to speak to the people.

"Gather round, folks, gather round. I am Jake. I will be showing you around this here town that I hope you will make your new home. We are close to the mines for those of you coming to make your fortune, and I can arrange a pack team for you. We leave first thing in the morning. For those wishing to settle here in town, I am the man to take care of this. I also take care of postings if you want to send word to loved ones back home. I will give you a tour of the town. You will see parts of the town are being rebuilt due to a recent fire. With better construction and a new pump for our firehouse, this will not happen again. Rest assured, good people. As you can see, new businesses are being built as we speak. Come along."

Jake stepped out onto the street and waved his arm for the crowd to follow. A marching band struck up a tune at the end of the procession. Caniday fell in with the group.

As they walked down the center of the street, Jake pointed out the building under construction. "This here's gonna be dry goods and millinery store," he called out, pointing to his right. "Now, to the left here we got your meat market to replace one lost to the fire. Over here," he pointed, "will be a carpenter, and there a shoemaker. You got the jailhouse and courthouse coming up over here, complete with a hanging post to the side of the building, a building not consumed in the fire. Here you have the coroner and undertaker's quarters. Let's hope you don't need his services too soon." Laughter broke out in the crowd.

"Keep it moving, folks, we have a lot to see yet, keep it moving," Jake called out, spinning around to continue his speech. "Now, getting into the outskirts of town toward the port, which is the main source of import to these parts, I might add, we have a brick-layer, and here is a liquor store. Across the street we have a fine hotel, The Golden Lion. A new one just down from it too, so we'll have two in town. I forgot to mention that at the other end of town we have the African Church and at this end we have the Reverend Crow's house of worship. Here's your blacksmith, and finally the tannery is over yonder. Just outside of town, we have sheep and a horse ranch run by the teamsters. There are cow farms, vineyards, and a medical clinic and drug dispensary at your disposal. We even have the state asylum for you nuts among us! This here is the end of our little tour, folks. Do you have any questions?"

A man stepped out from the crowd. "Where do we settle in for the night? My wife and I are road weary and hungry."

"I want to go to the mines right away!" shouted another voice from the crowd.

"I want to see the land that we heard was for sale to get a home-stead," cried another man.

"What about a bank? You didn't mention a bank. What about a postal express office?"

"Where's the saloon? I'm as dry as that desert we came across."

"Now then, let us go back to my establishment, and I can address those who have needs. The rest of you, pull your wagons in a circle on the land behind the Public House. That is where you will settle tonight, and we can start fresh in the morning."

Caniday stood silent and listened to the crowd. He had an idea of how to earn some money. As the crowd began thinning out and moving to the Public House, he walked up behind the man who wanted to go to the mines. "Mister, I can take you to the mines." he boldly stated.

The man turned around and looked down with a scrunched up face at this brown-skinned boy. "You? Why you're just a kid!"

Caniday stood proudly. "I am older than I look, sir, and I can take you to the mines, for a price."

"Okay, I don't know why I should trust you with this big task, especially you're an Injun. But I need to get rich fast and then skedaddle back home, so let's get my mule and get a-goin'," the man agreed.

Caniday followed the man back to his pack mule and horse. They started out of town toward the mines, the man on horseback and Caniday on the pack mule.

By late afternoon, they arrived at the foot of the Sierras and headed toward the Truckee River. The sun was sinking ever lower when they arrived at a place called Hang Town. The small encampment was all but deserted except for a few stragglers sitting around a campfire singing to a violin player's sad tune.

"Hello there, is this where I can search for gold?" The man asked at the campfire as he entered the camp.

"Howdy, stranger. You're in the right place, that's if'n you can find any here. Just don't steal a claim."

"The names Flannery," the man said and reached out his hand to shake.

"I'm Jeb, and this here's Jacob and James."

"Pleasure to be sure," said Flannery "Do you mind if I share your fire? I have vittles I can share with you all."

"Why not?" said Jeb. "Who's that you got wi'cha?"

"Why this here's my guide, brought me all the way from Stockton. What's your name kid?"

I am Caniday," he proudly stated.

"Well then, Caniday, go gather some more wood for this here fire."

Flannery pulled down his pack from the mule and gathered some beans and jerked meat. He put them all together in a pot and placed it on the fire.

Caniday came back with his arms full of kindling and let it fall into a pile near the logs that served as seats around the fire.

The group silently ate the meal, and when everyone had had their fill, Jacob picked up his violin and Jeb brought out a bottle of whiskey, passing it around as Jacob played and James danced a jig. A good time was had by all that night; even Caniday took his turn drinking the whiskey. As the night progressed, Jeb and Jacob began telling stories of what life in the mining camps was like. The hard work, the fights among the miners—including stabbings—and even a hanging. Also, they told about a pretty little Indian squaw that was a soiled dove.

Caniday didn't know what a soiled dove was, but his ears perked up when they mentioned an Indian squaw. He wanted to know more, because he figured it might be his mama. "What happened to the dove?" Caniday said, slurring his speech as he was not used to drinking whiskey.

"Why, you little dickens, you is too young to be wondering about such things," Flannery said as he ruffled Caniday's hair.

Flannery, Jeb, and Jacob all whooped with laughter. Jacob hic-coughed. Caniday stared at the fire, and Jacob fell off the log, passed out where he lay.

"Well the music has died, so I guess we should turn in," Jeb said as he stood up, stretched, and yawned.

Flannery went to his bundle of supplies. He pulled out two blankets and handed one to Caniday.

Caniday took the blanket from Flannery. I am searching for my mama. She was stolen by two white men from our village. Can we go to the place where the dove is?"

"Hey, kid, you can stay on and be my helper if you like. We may just head on up that way."

Caniday nodded. He set his blanket next to the fire and fell fast asleep, thoughts of his mother filling his head.

Caniday and Flannery mined the Truckee River for a while and then decided to move to new diggings. They traveled to the Calaveras River branch, where they heard there was a strike. Caniday worked alongside Flannery and gave him his findings minus a few small nuggets of gold he kept for himself. After they could no longer find gold, they traveled farther up the Calaveras. Eventually they reached the camp where Mr. York, Molly, and Lilly were staying.

One night, Flannery paid for the company of Molly. Along with his five minutes of pleasure from Molly, he grilled her for information about the Indian squaw who had lived there for a time.

When he returned to his camp after his visit with Molly, Flannery woke up the sleeping Caniday. "Hey, kid, this is the camp where the squaw was staying...the 'soiled dove' that you are looking for. She stole something from one of the other girls and was thrown into the river. If it was your mama, she may not still be alive. That river is treacherous. It would be hard for anyone to survive."

Caniday sat up on one elbow. "It could be my mama, and she could still be alive! But where would she be now?"

Flannery shrugged his shoulders and pulled his blanket up to his chin. "You have been a great help to me. I'm leaving to go back home tomorrow. You can ride back to Stockton with me in the morning." Flannery rolled over and in a few minutes his gentle snoring was the only sound in the still night.

Caniday lay back down, but sleep eluded him this night.

Flannery and Caniday arrive in Stockton by noon the next day. They went to the general store where the assay desk was. Flannery got his gold weighed and was paid in cash. Caniday was next to have his gold weighed. The assayer put the scale he had just used to weigh Flannery's gold under the counter and pulled out a different scale, the one used to measure any nonwhite person's gold. This did not go unnoticed by Caniday, but he said nothing.

Flannery said his good-byes. Caniday stood in the street outside the general store and watched him ride out of town.

Caniday put his hand in his shirt pocket. He felt the coins he had received from his gold mining. He pulled one out and held it up to reflect the shine of the sun. He realized that he would never be able to purchase goods from the general store or the restaurant. The money was useless to him. How he loved shiny things.

He was hungry, so he decided on a trip to Colonel Jackson's ranch. He loved looking at that glass horse. He would be back in town by nightfall.

The next morning was judgment day in town. All the people were gathered next to the jailhouse for the hanging of the bank robber. The circuit judge held a trial that lasted only long enough for the several witnesses to give their testimony and convict the robber-murderer to hang by the neck until dead. The crowd seemed excited to see the hanging.

The prisoner was led to the platform by Sheriff Dodd, Otis, a preacher, and the editor of the *Stockton Bee*. The rope was placed around the neck of the convicted man, and when the order was given to pull the lever that released the floor upon which the convict stood, he spoke his last words: "God forgive me!"

The judge nodded his head, and Otis pulled the lever that opened the hatch where the convicted man stood. There was a gasp from the crowd as the convict's body fell through and jerked and bounced until he dangled motionless.

All eyes were diverted to a thunderous sound entering from the edge of town, coming toward them. It was Colonel Jackson, riding tall in the saddle and followed by fifty men on horseback. The men on horses marched in a regimented row. All fifty had on dark grey pantaloons with a scarlet stripe up the seam of the leg, blue coats with scarlet trimmings, and a cap upon their heads.

The colonel stepped down from his horse and climbed the stairway that led to the hanging platform. Holding up his leather-gloved hand, he looked around at the crowd and began to speak.

"People of the fine town of Stockton. Are you afraid of the thievery that is going on under our very noses? Our horses and cattle stolen right out from under us? When we lay our heads down to sleep at night, are we safe in our own homes? Or might our wives and daughters be carried off by savages?"

The crowd shouted in agreement.

"Lawlessness in this town is now at an end," he continued. "I have taken it upon myself, with the approval of the United States government, to form a vigilante committee. These fifty men under my command that you see before you are now the new law here. We will rid the land of the savages that raid our livestock and steal our food stores. I vow to make this town into the great place we deserve. Furthermore, I vow to capture every Indian within one hundred miles of here to be placed in a reservation and keep you and your families and new settlers safe! There, the United States government has agreed to provide them with food and house them where they can live their lives and we can continue to live our lives in peace."

The crowd was whipped up into a frenzy. The band began to play, and all cheered as hats were thrown into the air. The crowd whooped and hollered.

Colonel Jackson raised his hands again to quiet the crowd. "For those Indians refusing to go to the reservation and the renegades that continue to raid our lands, we will go after them, and they will pay the consequences. To help rid these parts of the savages, I will pay two dollars for every scalp you bring me!"

The crowd went wild with excitement.

Caniday blended into the crowd and slowly backed up. When he was behind the crowd, he ran to his canvas shelter hiding place behind the jailhouse.

The headline of the *Stockton Bee* the next day read, "Rid the Land of Riff-Raff!" and the edition sold like hotcakes.

Caniday laid low for a few days. The sheriff's office was busy with men bringing scalps in.

One man's voice was heard complaining, "Sheriff, my ranch hand, an Injun, was scalped right on my property. I want to be paid for losing a good worker!"

"Now, Sam, I ain't gonna pay you for losing one of your help. It was just an Injun."

After hiding out for two days, Caniday got restless. He also ran out of food and was hungry. He started walking out of town where he felt safest. It was getting too dangerous to stay in town. He thought it might be time to go the reservation that he was hearing about.

LUNA

Each night, Luna wandered down to the port, where she sold her body for a bottle of whiskey. After a night with several men, she stumbled into the tented church late into the night to sleep if off.

Her coughing fits were taking over her body until she was finding it increasingly harder to get a willing participant. Even the drunkest of sailors or the vilest of filthy vagrants did not want to touch her. Some nights, she had to scrounge the empty bottles that were cast aside in the refuse behind the saloons.

One such night, she was in the alley behind the saloon when a man cornered her. "Say, you're an Injun, ain'tcha?"

Luna spun around to see a big, burly fur-coated man. His eyes were like black coals. He stood with a grin on his face, his brown teeth poking out of a straggly, matted beard. He held his arms out to block the exit of the alley. Luna stood frozen, her eyes looking for a way to escape.

"You want a good time?" Luna asked sheepishly. "I could make you feel real good for a bottle of whiskey." Luna sashayed up to the man. She could smell whiskey and tobacco on the bearded man. He grabbed Luna by the wrist and spun her around.

"No need to get rough, mister," Luna screamed as she was pushed to her knees, facing away from the man.

She was used to being manhandled by clients, but she was puzzled at this action. She'd had some strange requests from men, but this felt different. She shivered and became frightened. The man grabbed her by her hair. She struggled and spun around, and the reflection of the full moon shone for a moment on the blade of a knife in the man's hand. Luna reached up to pull his hand free of her hair. That was when she saw that he had a large knife in his hand and intended to cut her. At first, she thought he was going to cut her throat, and then when a drop of blood ran down her face, the reality of what was about to happen hit her. She was being scalped!

Luna let out a bloodcurdling scream.

"Hey!" Luna heard a man's voice call out and she saw Joseph, the Jamesons' helper from the church. He ran up to the man and punched him in the nose, causing the man to let go of Luna's hair. She sprang up and kicked the bearded man square in the groin.

The bearded man howled in agony and fell to his knees and then onto the ground as he rolled around holding his groin.

Joseph took Luna by the hand and they ran out of the alley. "Mabel sent me out to find you; you are not safe. It looks like I found you just in time. There is a price for that lovely scalp on your head."

Luna wiped the blood from her forehead and looked at it. "Thank you for saving me."

Joseph and Luna got back to the tented church. Mabel greeted them and thanked Joseph. She got some water and torn cloth strips to tend to Luna's cut forehead.

Mabel took Luna's hands in hers and looked her in the eye. "Pastor Jameson and I are worried about your safety. There is a price on your head, and there will be more men after you. You can stay here, but we can only protect you so much. I think you may have to go to the reservation with your people. That may be the only safe place for you to go."

Luna looked up at Mabel. Tears started to well up in her eyes. "I cannot go to the reservation. I am ashamed. Luna sobbed now, holding her face in her hands. Then another coughing fit started; it seemed as it would never cease this time.

Mabel called out to Joseph. "Go fetch Doc Johansen!"

"Yes, ma'am," Joseph said as he hurried out the door of the tented church.

Mabel got a blanket, wrapped Luna up in it, and brought her some hot tea. She used one of the torn cloths to wipe the blood from Luna's lips that she had coughed up. She held up a tin cup with water.

"Drink this; it will soothe you," Mabel said as she assisted Luna in drinking from the cup.

CANIDAY

Caniday woke to Colonel Jackson's voice on the other side of the sheriff's wall. "Sheriff Dodd, we rounded up those cattle wrestlers on the north side of town, the ones responsible for raiding over at the Smiths' place. Caught them red-handed. Some of the boys are bringing them in—they'll be here shortly."

"That's fine work you battalion boys are doing," said Sheriff Dodd. "Putting all those Injuns on reservations. That village up yonder that was raiding all the ranches was a real thorn in my side. Now that sure makes my job a lot easier. Say, how is the rounding up of those renegade Injuns going along?"

"It's going fine. There are a few renegades who refuse to comply. They won't go to the reservation. We have ways of persuading them. It is in their best interest to go peacefully."

"That's just great, Colonel. And how is that wife of yours? I hear she is back home now."

"Yep, she is, but she is still so delicate. She had a good rest at the asylum. There's some good doctors over there. I hope she will be better out on the ranch with all that fresh air. She still insists that she saw an Injun there that time. I have seen that little injun boy running around town. But I'll be damned if I can catch him. He's slick that one even for a kid. I'm beginning to believe her. If I catch any savages on my land, I'm going to take the necessary steps to insure that they never think about setting foot anywhere they don't belong ever again...if you get my drift."

"I get it." Sheriff Dodd let out a belly laugh. "I'll see you later, Edward."

Caniday heard the door of the jailhouse slam. He lay down and settled in for the night. Very early the next morning, the grumbling of Caniday's stomach woke him. He was so hungry. It was still dark, so he felt it was safe to sneak out of town to Col Jackson's ranch and get some food. His grandfather had taught him to hunt small game, but there was no game left to hunt the new settlers saw to that. So he had to raid ranches to get food. It was not difficult walking in the early hours of a new day. The horizon was a light hue of pink and gold. He had been here many times. He felt at home out in the open range of the field. He heard a coyote howl in the distance and another in harmony. The only obstacles were cows here and there. He could see them in the shadows and avoided them.

It was easy for him to keep going back to the Jackson ranch, the food was easy to get to and there was never anyone around to impede his thievery.

He reached the Jackson ranch and went to the food storage. It had a new lock on it that he could not penetrate. He walked around to the other side of the house, being careful not to be seen. He stopped to listen for voices but there were none. He saw an open window and peeked inside. All was still. The glow from the fire in the fireplace cast a shadow that was inviting to him, and he slipped into the open window. Once inside, he tiptoed and stopped to listen. Hearing no sound, he breathed a sigh of relief. He saw some apples and grapes in a bowl on a table and helped himself. The sweet taste of the apple mixed with the grapes was sumptuous to him, and he stuffed his mouth full. Then he put an apple and some grapes in his shirt. Next to the bowl of fruit was a platter with bread and some cheese. He took a big bite of the bread and cheese, letting them mingle in his mouth. He tore off more bread and a slab of cheese and put them in his shirt with the fruit for later. The fire drew his attention, and he walked over to it, holding out his hands toward the dancing embers. It felt so good. The glimmer of the fire caught his eye on the glass horse statue, the one he had seen before. He picked it up, noticing how heavy it was, and held it up to the firelight. The colors were magnificent and so mesmerizing that he got lost in its beauty.

"Ah HA!" a woman's voice rang out, breaking the spell. "I knew you were real! They didn't believe me but here you are! Get out! Get out, I say, you filthy savage! Help! *Help!*" She screamed louder and louder.

Caniday, caught off guard, looked in the direction of the voice. There stood Mrs. Jackson, halfway down the staircase in a white nightgown.

He dropped the glass horse and it shattered into a hundred pieces that flew in all directions. He stood frozen for a moment. Realizing the trouble he was in, he ran to an open window. He leaped toward the open window, which was not the one he had entered through. There was a round table draped with a white lace cloth over it that he had to scramble over to get out the window. On the table was a gas lantern. He reached the window, but not without first knocking over the table.

The gas lantern crashed to the floor and burst into flames. The gas spread the flame to the lace tablecloth and the carpet. The flames reached the curtains, and soon the hungry fire grabbed hold of anything and everything, including the wooden table and stairs that Mrs. Jackson was standing on. Her sleeping gown caught fire, and she ran screaming up the stairs. The flames grew and overtook her gown. In minutes, she and the house were engulfed in flames.

Caniday jumped up and out the window on the other side of the room. He landed in the dirt outside of the house, jumped up, and started running. The apple and grapes inside of his shirt were crushed, making an oozing mess. The bread and cheese stayed intact, but they eventually fell out as he ran.

Flames and thick black smoke were billowing into the sky by now, and men working in the outer yards of the ranch saw this and ran toward the house. Neighboring ranchers saw the smoke and came riding up on horses to help. A bucket brigade was started from the lake next to the house, but it was to no avail. All was lost.

LUNA

Dr. Johansen straightened up as he removed the stethoscope from his ears. "This is one sick woman. Her body is ravaged by malnourishment, an advanced case of syphilis, and consumption—any one of which could kill her. I'm afraid there is nothing I can do. I can give you some laudanum, which will make her comfortable. Unfortunately, that is all I can offer."

Mabel put a blanket on Luna as she lay on a cot at the tented church. She took the bottle from the doctor.

"Have her take this for discomfort," the doctor said as he put on his coat and walked toward the door.

"Thank you kindly, Doctor. I will be taking her to the reservation. I think she will be safe there among her people," Mabel said.

"Fine, but not for a few days; let her rest up some and gather some strength, if she can," ordered Dr. Johansen as he reached the entrance to the tent.

After a fitful night with Luna, Mabel whispered to Luna as she lay on the cot. "Luna, I have made arrangements for you to go to the reservation. It is best this way. I will be gone for a few days, as I have work to do at the asylum. You will be safe here until I return. Then Joseph will take you to the reservation. Here is your bottle of medicine from the doctor. Take it as you need it."

Mabel picked up her bag and went out the door, escorted by Joseph.

Luna awoke drenched in sweat. Her breathing was labored and short. She felt like she would suffocate if she didn't get some cool fresh air. She sat up, putting her legs over the side of the cot, and attempted to stand up. She fell back down onto the cot. The doorway was just a few short steps away, but the amount of energy it would take to get there was miles away. She desperately needed to get to that doorway. She lay back down on the cot and slipped into unconsciousness.

Opening her eyes, she gathered up the little strength she had and sat up. Putting her feet on the floor, she stood up again, this time holding onto the cot for support. Her knees wobbled as she took a small step in the direction of the doorway. The brown bottle of laudanum was in her hand. She took another step, this time on her own away from the support of the cot. Her legs too weak to hold her frail body, she fell to the floor, the brown bottle skittering a few feet away. She lay there for a few moments and then, gathering all the strength she possessed, she got up on her hands and knees and slowly inched toward the doorway, picking up the brown bottle along the way.

She reached the doorway barely able to breathe. She let the coolness of the fresh air wash over her. A few minutes later, Joseph pulled up in the wagon, back from taking Mabel to the asylum. He saw Luna lying at the entrance to the tented church, jumped down from the wagon, and ran to her. "What are you doing out of bed? You should be resting. Let me help you back to bed," Joseph said as he gently picked Luna up.

Luna, cradled in Joseph's arms, whispered with all the might she had left in her body. "No, please let me sit outside. I want to see the blue of the sky and feel the cool breeze on my face."

Joseph looked at Luna, her face pale and gaunt. He saw the light in her eyes dimming and granted her request. He turned around and set her down on the wood-planked walkway outside the entrance to the church, propping her up against the canvas wall. He grabbed a blanket and wrapped it around her shoulders. He opened the brown bottle and held it up to her lips. She smiled at him, nodded her head, and then slipped into unconsciousness.

Caniday tripped on a sagebrush and planted his face into the sandy dirt as he ran from the burning Jackson house. Getting back up, not missing a beat, he ran through the field and up a hill. When he got to the top of the hill, he hid behind a clump of tumbleweeds. He listened carefully, trying to ascertain if he had been followed

A lone horseman rode full speed away from the towering black smoke that could be seen for miles. Chasing after Caniday who he had seen ducking in the bushes. The horseman turned away from the direction to make it look like he was going away, only to turn full circle and see Caniday raise up out of the brush.

Thinking he had gotten away, Caniday stood to walk back to town. He lifted up his shirt and scraped up the smashed apple and grape bits that clung to his belly. He wasn't hungry anymore.

Caniday was surprised when along came a man behind him on horseback and lassoed him with a rope. "I got ya! Think you got away with burning that house, do you? I seen you running away from there. Well, you killed Mrs. Jackson and you're gonna pay! I'm taking you to the sheriff!" the man on horseback said.

The horseman jumped down off of his horse and wrapped the rope around and around him snugly, tying his arms to his side. Then he lifted Caniday up and threw him sideways across the horse. He got back up into the saddle and rode to town with lightning speed.

When the horseman reached town he stopped short at Sheriff Dodd's office. Pulling Caniday down from his horse, he carried him into the jailhouse and dropped him onto the floor in front of Sheriff Dodd's desk. He landed with a thud and bumped his head on the wooden floor.

"What have we got here?" asked the sheriff.

"Sheriff, Colonel Jackson's house just burnt down, burnt to the ground—with Mrs. Jackson inside. And this is the varmint that done it. I saw him running from the burning house with my own eyes."

Sheriff Dodd looked at Caniday. "Yes, a posse rode out there to help put out the fire. You say it burnt to the ground?" He looked down at him tied up and laying on the floor. "Well, son, what have you got to say?"

"I was hungry—I just needed something to eat."

Just then Deputy Otis walked into the office. "Sheriff, we couldn't save the Jacksons' house or Mrs. Jackson."

"Put him in the cell, Otis," the sheriff said as he tossed the keys to the deputy.

Otis pulled Caniday up, with the rope still tightly wound around him, jerking him roughly as he was led to the jail cell. Otis opened the cell door and untied the rope, and then he slammed the cell door with a loud clang. Otis, with a toothpick hanging out of the corner of his mouth, paused to stare at Caniday before he turned and walked away.

Caniday lay down on the bunk and stared at the ceiling of the jailhouse.

"Otis, you will stand guard tonight. Nobody gets into this jail-house. Do you understand? Nobody. I'm going to get some shut-eye. I'll be back at first light," commanded Sheriff Dodd.

"Nobody, sir," Otis replied.

Sheriff Dodd walked out of the jailhouse to an angry crowd of men waiting in the street along with the editor of the *Stockton Bee*. The men in the angry mob were dressed in various colors of check-ered shirts with denim and cotton pants, leather boots, and straw or felt hats. Several of the men held up coiled ropes. The mob consisted of town folk as well as farmers and ranchers from the outskirts of town. Also store keepers, livery workers, and saloon keepers were there.

Leading the mob was Colonel Jackson himself, followed by several members of his vigilante committee. He stood in front of Sheriff Dodd. "Now look here, Sheriff, we want justice to be served here, and we want it *now*! That savage killed my wife and burned my house. So just step aside."

"Now, Colonel, I know you are upset. I'm sorry for your loss, and I know you want instant justice. But I am the law here, and I say we wait until the judge arrives; we will handle this by the law. I have sent for the judge already."

The crowd started to disperse, grumbling and mumbling. Colonel Jackson stared at Sheriff Dodd and then turned and walked away.

The editor of the *Stockton Bee* stepped up to the sheriff with pencil and paper in hand. "Sheriff Dodd, can you give me some information so I can keep the people of this fair town apprised of the situation?"

"You know as much as I do. There will be a trial, fair and square. You can tell that to your readers."

The editor persisted. "Sheriff Dodd, do you think it is fair to arrest a boy such as this, a mere child, and hold him up to the law as an adult? He's but ten or twelve years of age. We have institutions for wayward boys. Wouldn't it be more fair to send him to such a place, given the fact that he is only a child?"

"We will let the circuit judge decide his fate. He will arrive in the morning." Sheriff Dodd stuck a cigar in his mouth and lit it with a match he pulled from his britches. "Good day, sir," he said and then walked across the street to the saloon.

He entered the saloon and walked up to the bar. "Give me a bottle of your best whiskey and two glasses." He then placed a few coins on the bar. Picking up the bottle and glasses, he walked over to an empty table in the back of the bar and poured himself a shot. He then filled the other glass and pushed it across the table to an empty chair.

Colonel Jackson walked into the saloon and stood in the doorway. Looking around and noticing the sheriff, he stormed over to the table. "I was expecting to see you, Colonel Jackson," the sheriff said as he pushed the glass of whiskey toward him.

"Please have a seat." The sheriff pointed to the empty chair across from him.

Colonel Jackson pulled out the chair and sat down. He picked up the glass of whiskey and chugged it down, slamming the glass on the table.

"Before you say anything, I want to tell you how truly sorry I am for your loss." He poured another whiskey for himself and refilled Jackson's glass.

"I want justice for my wife's death!" Colonel Jackson said through clenched teeth.

"Listen, Edward, I know how you feel. I want justice too…not just a slap on the wrist for this kid. If he robs, steals, and murders at this young age, he will probably rob, steal and kill again. But I can't just hand him over to you and your vigilantes. The newspaper is all over this, and with it being almost time for reelection, I need this job. So tomorrow I will be taking the boy to the courthouse. Only problem is I have only myself and my deputy, Otis—not nearly enough protection for the lad." The sheriff winked at Colonel Jackson.

The colonel slammed his shot of whiskey and set the glass upside down on the table. Sliding his chair away from the table, he looked down at Sheriff Dodd and gave him a wink. Then he turned and walked out of the saloon.

The town was all abuzz with the anticipation of the judge's arrival. The sun was barely up, and people were filling the seats of the courtroom. There were so many people that the overflow spilled out into the streets.

Caniday was awakened by the sound of keys clanging open the cell door.

"On your feet!" Deputy Otis commanded.

Caniday complied and stood up. His hands were tied in front with a rope because his wrists were too small for a pair of irons.

The deputy pointed to the door of the jailhouse with the rifle in his hands.

Caniday walked out into the sunshine followed by the armed deputy, Caniday's shadow casting a false figure of a full grown man on the dirt street. It was a short walk, hampered by the throngs of people milling around to see the trial. As they went by, some men shouted at him, calling him a murderer and holding up coils of rope.

Mabel, just returning from the state asylum and seeing the spectacle, pushed her way to the front. "What kind of human beings are we to send a boy to trial? Do we not all deserve a chance at redemption and salvation?"

The deputy pushed past Mabel and the crowd of people holding onto Caniday's arm, dragging him along to the entrance of the courtroom. The sheriff arrived, and he, along with Colonel Jackson and his vigilante committee, entered the courtroom.

Sheriff Dodd stood at the front of the courtroom, facing the people. "There is a slight delay in the arrival of the judge this morning. He won't be here for another hour or two. Deputy Otis, put the prisoner in the chamber adjacent to this one, off to the side, and hold him there until the arrival of the judge."

Deputy Otis led Caniday into the little chamber off to the side of the courtroom. Sheriff Dodd turned, mumbling something about some forgotten papers, and hurried out of the courtroom.

Colonel Jackson watched as the sheriff left the room. He motioned with his arms for the group of vigilantes to follow him. The crowd started whooping and hollering, and they gathered steam as they burst into the little room where Caniday sat with Deputy Otis.

"It's time for you to pay for your crime, varmint!" Colonel Jackson said as he grabbed Caniday by the arms and flung him into the angry mob. Deputy Otis stood aside, allowing the crowd to take Caniday. "Take him to the hanging post!"

"Yeah!" cried the crowd. "Hang him!"

The mob, whipped up into a frenzy, snatched the bewildered Caniday up by his arms. Realizing that the crowd was taking him to the hanging post and that he was not going to get a trial, he began to resist. Several men in the mob grabbed Caniday by the arms and legs as he kicked and flailed with all of his might trying to get away.

"Help! Sheriff, where are you?" Caniday's voice could scarcely be heard above the shouts of the mob.

The crowd of people outside the courtroom stepped aside like the parting of the sea to allow the five men, led by Colonel Jackson, to pass. The crowd followed them to the hanging post. The men climbed up the stairs with the struggling Caniday. At the top of the hanging post, a rope with a noose was thrown over the top post. The noose was placed around Caniday's neck and cinched tight. The crowd cheered.

Colonel Jackson stepped up to Caniday. "You are found guilty of the death of one Mrs. Shirley Jackson and the burning of property. You are hereby sentenced to death for your crimes." The crowd cheered.

Caniday stood defiantly and looked at the crowd with contempt. "It was an accident. I didn't mean to do it. I was just hungry."

Colonel Jackson nodded his head to a vigilante, who pulled the lever. Caniday fell through the hole in the platform. He snapped and jerked, his feet kicking and flailing. Then he hung motionless.

LUNA

Mabel did not want to witness the travesty of justice that was going on with the town's people. She ran to her church. As she got closer to the church, she saw Luna sitting outside of the tented church and ran to her.

Luna was fading in and out of consciousness. Mabel could see that the end was near.

"Luna, let me take you inside. Let me make you more comfortable." Mabel started to lift Luna.

"No, no, let me die here. I just heard the call of a coyote. It spoke to me. Its sound was like my son, Caniday. I heard him calling to me." Luna gasped a few labored breaths and then lay still.

A few days later, the following story ran in the *San Francisco Bulletin*:

> May 31, 1859. A few days ago, in Stockton, a little Indian boy who set fire to the ranch of Colonel Jackson, head of the vigilante committee, was taken from the custody of Sheriff Dodd by a number of citizens and hanged. The sheriff had taken him to the courthouse for trial and left him in a room adjoining the courtroom, and while absent for a few minutes, the boy was taken by the mob. It is this editor's opinion that this is really horrible and reflects no credit to the parties concerned. This newspaper condemns the act in a very severe manner by alluding to it in "eloquent silence." The boy was but twelve or fifteen years of age. Although the real age of the boy is rumored to have been more like ten years of age. What good will the hanging of this stripling accomplish? Will it deter other Indian boys from committing similar acts? If so, the act is defensible. If not, appreciating the magnitude of his crime, is very true; but why not let him be hung in a legal manner? There is no danger of his escaping.

Author's note: This is an actual article from the *Bulletin*. The only thing changed in this story was the real name of Colonel Edward Stevenson to Colonel Edward Jackson.

www.ingramcontent.com/pod-product-compliance
Lightning Source LLC
Chambersburg PA
CBHW070925130626
46555CB00001B/289